((comma))

,

For Olive and Ann

PR 1307 .C54 2002

Comma

First published in Great Britain in 2002 by
Comma Press
Founder and Editor: Ra Page
Assistant Editor: Sarah-Jane Eyre
Distributed by Carcanet Press
www.carcanet.com

A CIP catalogue record of this book is available from the British Library

ISBN 1-85754-685-7
The publisher gratefully acknowledges assistance from the Arts Council of England
(North West Arts), and the assistance of *City Life* magazine.

Set in Monotype Garamond by XL Publishing Services, Tiverton
Printed and Bound in England by SRP Ltd, Exeter

contents

introduction

"There are, in our existence, spots of time"

The Prelude, Bk XII

The many attempts to define or distinguish the short story, beyond saying 'short stories are short', have, in the much-scribbled margins of the genre, occasionally sounded a bit desperate. 'At once a parable and a slice of life,' begins Kay Boyle's definition of the form, 'at once symbolic and real, both a valid picture of some phase of experience, and a sudden illumination of one of the perennial moral and psychological paradoxes which lie at the heart of *la condition humaine.*' A little needy perhaps? Jorge Luis Borges' contribution, 'unlike the novel, the short story may be, for all purposes, *essential*' may be, for all purposes, well meant but smacks of the same underlying inferiority complex.

It's not surprising. The short story has suffered a stream of body-blows over the last two hundred years, starting with a need to be entirely reborn in the face of the early nineteenth century novel (despite predating the novel, of course, by centuries). Then there was the penury of the mid-nineteenth century, when it lived by its wits in the literary gutter - namely American magazine culture and the pulp-genres of horror, early detective fiction, and Poe's embryonic science fiction. Even when the masters of the form eventually stepped forward - Chekhov, Joyce, Henry James, Kafka, Kipling and Lawrence - they did so in a free and easy manner, writing generous, unambiguously *long* short stories that invited the question as to whether they were shorts at all. Since then, the sheer weight of marginalia attracted by the form - the ubiquitous Raymond Carver dissertation that no postgrad department seems to be without - can hardly have helped. It's become a test-tube for critical theorists to hold up against the light of Chekhov, testing it against the Litmus paper of Carver; and, worst of all, a guinea pig for editors. Whether you're reading Philip Stevick's experimental *Anti-Story* anthology (1962), with its rejection of 'mimetic unities' in favour of non-narrative tone-poems, or Nic Blincoe and Matt Thorne's regressive *All Hail the New Puritans* (2000), with its Dogmé-style call for narrative simplicity – you are, despite appearances, being proselytised about fiction *generally*, not short fiction in particular; the short story is only there as a cross-section of what the editor thinks is or should be happening with the novel. Indeed, at no point in Blincoe and Thorne's editorial manifesto is there a single reference to the short story - though it does manage to commit an entire commandment (Point Six) to the scourge of 'elaborate punctuation'.

Add to this the indifference of themed anthologies and the passivity of retrospective ones ('Welsh Short Stories from 1960 to 1980', and the like) and you begin to wonder what the short story's done to deserve this. Of course, most of these afflictions are commercial in origin. Any publisher will tell you, you can't *give* short stories away. But that isn't to say that what the form needs is a grant (to allow short story writers to work at it full-time), or some kind of preservation order (to dissuade them from being converted into novelists); many of the best shorts have been written at odd moments by novelists and dramatists merely having a day off, or by writers like D. H. Lawrence who was both a novelist and a poet.

Most of all, there certainly doesn't seem to be any need to 'define' the damn thing... And yet, to introduce a new collection of short stories without at least having a go, seems unsporting.

Let's start at the top. If we were to inspect them with a clipboard, successful short stories would no doubt score highly in certain boxes: unity (of tone, motif or theme) - tick; sharpness (of language or characterisation) - tick; circularity (of plot devices or metaphor) - tick tick tick. Listed like this though, it's easy to argue that all these features are, in themselves, merely functions of brevity, consequences of conciseness, side-effects of succinctness. Short stories are short stories because they're short. Endgame.

Try again, this time stretching the argument out a little to cover a wider spectrum of forms, including poetry as well as the novel - assuming, of course, that the short story falls somewhere in between.

Coleridge once observed that the difference between reading poetry and reading prose is that you can read prose lying down, but for poetry you have to be sitting up. A more helpful distinction here might be that you can read prose in your head, whilst you can only read poetry with your lips moving. By this I mean you have to read it *as if* you're reading it out loud. This has nothing to do with the history of verse - the usual guff about oral origins - only its on-going concern with the very physicality of speech, the act on intoning, the machinery of the mouth. Consciously or unconsciously, a kind of silent performance, a textual dumbshow, occurs in every reading of a poem. In verse, voice is the key.

Indeed, it extends beyond just lips moving, to lips *not* moving. The mouth stalled, slightly open. This is precisely the common ground that the poem shares with the short story: the gaps. In poetry these are the verse-breaks, the line-breaks, the Anglo-Saxon caesuras, the hanging fourth foot in lines four and sometimes two of the traditional ballad stanza; they are the levers and cogs of the mouth, the anchors and pulleys that work even the most modern, most 'unperformable' poems.

In short stories, the gaps are less uniform. Ostensibly they're the before and after; the back-story we're never told which, if the author's timing is right, we don't need to be told; and the outcome, the ever-after, the next episode in the protagonist's evidently episodic existence. Or rather they're the *lack* of an existence either side. Their abruptness is always structured, however, and in a good story, designed specifically for their contribution. In Clare Pollard's 'Kirsten vs the City', for instance, the sudden unscrewing of focus at the end brings the moral indifference that's been backgrounding the story suddenly skittering into view. You couldn't do this in a novel.

Nor are these gaps restricted to just book-ending the short. In commissioning these stories I've tried to encourage the breaking up of narratives and, with this, a precise, strategic use of internal pausing. The breaks in Emma Unsworth's 'Doppelgänger' hint at, without signposting, switches in perspective. In Paul Morley's 'Decision Time', they enact a referential ping-pong between addresser and addressee. In Wayne Clews' 'Going to the Dogs', the breaks between each inventory stare out at the reader with the same apathetic *ennui* the narrator speaks with. In 'Girl with Leaves in Her Mouth' and 'Clocks and Faces', the crepuscular tone is itself a kind of silence. And even when the stops and starts seem conventional, as in the frames around Amanda Dalton's 'Pictures', the fact is they couldn't be sustained in a novel. David Constantine is the one author who's consciously cottoned on to this natural fissuring of short writing, fighting against it by avoiding paragraph breaks and standard punctuation, in pursuit of fluidity. But either way, the pressure towards rhythmic, internal pausing is there.

As any actor will tell you, these little silences are what really *make* a performance; they are the momentary spaces that the audience fills, or during which it catches up. In a good comedian, they're that sense of timing we call 'natural', instinctively sharing it ourselves. Or - to leap-frog into yet another artform - they are the blank expressions at the climax of a great movie. When the director Michael Curtiz framed the closing scene in *Casablanca*, the one with Ingrid Bergman's swooning gaze from under that enormously brimmed hat, he famously asked her to let her face be completely expressionless. Yet to us, of course, who've painted-in what have become our own emotions, to us she's so passionate!

These blank canvases, these hesitations are the spots of time, that appear within the spots of time.

Hence 'Comma'.

By hard-wiring a text with the sheer physicalities of speech, with an in-built performance, what the poet and the short story writer are primarily doing is making their work public. Not garret-bound or graveyard-seated, nor ivory towered or arcane, but common. Whether it's with the licks and loops of alliteration, or the intuitive timing of a hesitation, they're not shutting the world out through specialism or technique, they're letting it rush in.

In contrast to this physicality, the novel has one major counter: plot. Granted these demarcations are relatively fluid - there are singular, 'poetic' novels like *Moby Dick*, whose sheer size seems to add to their singularity, just as there are great, sprawling 'novelistic' poems - but generally the novel has narrative, and in abundance. Likewise, the 'story' half of the short story's eternally inadequate nomenclature isn't there without reason either; the short story has plot too (if rather a short one).

Unlike the poem's public voice, though, what plot can only ever be is subjective, private; one author's moral or amoral, systematic or chaotic understanding of how things are, one author's world-view pasted onto what he or she claims is *our* world; a place presided over by the author-as-God, or otherwise populated by the author's clones - not unlike the scene in Spike Jonze's *Being John Malkovich*, where the restaurant is full of people sporting only John Malkovich's face, and the cross-table chit-chat translates only as 'Malkovich, Malkovich, Malkovich...'

Despite their respective sizes, the poem, I would argue, is surprisingly expansive, the novel in part reductive; one trying to find the world in a grain of sand (or rather letting the linguistic world rush into it), the other trying to build the world, or at least a few castles, out a whole beachful of the stuff.

Which brings me to my point (I knew I'd left it here somewhere). If voice and plot distance poems and novels, mutually, the only thing that neither have a proper purchase on, despite their respective claims, and the only thing that can stabilise the outward and inward forces of verse and novel-writing, is character.

An early attempt to define the short story that's often picked-on is Frank O'Connor's, in his collection of essays, *The Lonely Voice* (1962). Traditional short stories, he claimed, invariably featured 'outlawed figures' striving to escape from 'submerged population groups', rather than 'normal' characters - a concern O'Connor reserves for the novel. Short stories are also, he notes, natively romantic, individualistic and intransigent. All of which can be said of countless novels, we all chorus - Graham Greene's *The Power and the Glory*, to pick just one - and all of which, some would argue, are *intrinsic* to the novel. The critic James Wood believes it a duty of the novel to lead the reader and the protagonist 'deep into language' and therein 'abandon us'... No fitting into society as a whole there, then.

But maybe we should give O'Connor the benefit of the doubt here, or at least follow his hunch a little further. His sense that characters are somehow stronger in short stories than novels, more individual, I'd actually take a step further. Not only are the characters more vivid in short stories, they're more *real* (classing the 'realest' protagonists -

Meursault, Gregor Samsa, Hemingway's Old Man - as the stars of short stories rather than that non-species the *nouvelle*). It is the conviction of our first impressions, as readers, that short story characters draw their strength from, and this conviction is as close to 'living off the page' as they will get.

A few weeks before going to press, the author of the opening story here, Michael Symmons Roberts, told me he had successfully begun to pull the piece apart and re-wire it into a novel. I was delighted. The crime photographer at the heart of his story fascinated me, this image of him hanging out pictures without a fixer, to fix a limit on his voyeurism. There had to be so much more to him! My taste for him was whetted. But isn't this the wonder of the short? The appetite being heightened by being denied? If there's a writer capable keeping the character alive, or *as* alive, for the duration of a novel, it's Michael Symmons Roberts. But you do wonder how A Year in the Life would stand up to A Day in the Life.

For the time being, and for the duration of this collection, days in the life are what we have. Of the fifteen writers here, none is by profession, or even by hobby, a short story writer. They are, however, day-trippers. Wild, hedonistic, born-to-interlop day trippers: poets finding their lines suddenly carrying on to the edge of the page; novelists gripped by ideas that arrive whole, unattenuated. Even journalists and playwrights discover a different kind of voice, here, as if sounding out the echoes of an unfamiliar building.

As the first publication by Comma, we hope this book will be followed by novels and other longer works next year, perhaps by some of the authors already featured; but we are also committed to an annual anthology of short stories, compiled without political or demographic themes, and selected only on the basis of quality. It's a long sentence, but with Comma we hope to make it longer.

Ra Page
October, 2002

Ambulance-Chaser

Michael Symmons Roberts

A was written in blood where the bodies were found. It was paint, but the story went round town that it was blood. More than that, the story said Marie had dipped a finger in her gaping chest, to write a message on the concrete car park wall. She had finished the first letter, then collapsed.

The first letter of what? Her friends said it must have been the name of the killer. She was writing ADAM SLIGO, but her life ran out at A. Her sister Ally clung to the idea that it was ALLY I LOVE YOU, or ALLY DON'T WORRY. There was even a stupid theory that it wasn't A at all, that she was desperate and unable to shout, that she struggled to the wall and tried to write HELP in her own blood. It was really H, but she was so weak that the uprights fell into an A.

A few people knew that it was paint, and knew it had nothing to do with Marie. The police who were second on the scene were certain she had never left the car. The shots were fired at close range through the windscreen of Jake's old blue BMW. Jake and Marie both died in their seats. All the blood, and both victims, stayed inside the car.

I had evidence that Marie didn't write the A. I got there first as always. I had to get my work done before it was all cleared up. When I arrived, they were both dead, and in the background of my shots the wall is clean.

Proof counts for nothing unless it's your own proof. I've

thought a lot about this. I could have had one of my pictures blown up to billboard size and stuck it on the town hall. The red paint could have been sent for analysis, and the results bellowed through a megaphone by a man in a white coat. It wouldn't change a thing for those who thought Marie had left a final, cryptic message.

Far from fading, as the weeks passed, the story grew. A lot of people in this town needed some last word from her, some warning or consolation, something left behind for them. So I kept quiet about what I knew.

And what I knew was this: in the days after the murder, someone took a can of red paint and daubed a letter A at the crime scene. From the look of it, they used a hand rather than a brush. It was a mess, not a message. End of story.

*

It's a map-maker's term. I like to say I live on the edge of the edgelands. My flat turns its back on all the houses. My windows gaze across car-crushers, gasometers, hypermarkets, sewageworks - a mile-long no-man's land between streets and fields.

I can't work out how there was a fatal smash out there. My best guess is joy-riders up from London for the night, looking for a race-track with no speed cameras.

I make good time, since all the roads are clear. In the evenings, these business parks return to plan – a grid of tarmac strips, right-angle turns, green mounded roundabouts. The police channel's on as I drive, and their nearest car is still five miles back. This is easy.

I think of Fellig – the master – the only ambulance-chaser in New York to have a police radio fitted in his own car. What am I talking about? The only one ever. The ambulances had to chase him. He got to the smashes, fires, murders, so fast they'd barely happened. That's why the girls on the radio called him Weejee. He

2

was so quick he must be getting tip-offs from the dead.

But I'm quick too. Especially on my home turf. The edgelands are at their best tonight. The late sun picks out warehouses and offices – two breeds of building, one all metal, hunched and sealed; one all glass, evolved to live on light. I turn left past Collegiate Insurance, but on the hinge of the turn, the sun hits the mirrored face of the Collegiate Tower like a colossal flash-gun. Everything goes black, then through purple and magenta. In the seconds it takes to slow down and get my vision back, I hit something.

My eyes clear, and I see a big dog slouching away. Its coat is flashing in the sun, prismatic, almost dazzling. But its coat is outshone by its amber eyes. It breaks into a run, and slips between two warehouses.

My little accident has brought me within a car's length of the old BMW. It's in the middle of a big concrete courtyard walled on three sides by metal-shuttered warehouses. A dead end. I steer around the car, and circle it once. There's no-one around. No other car, and the body of this one is rusty but intact. It doesn't look like a crash. Only the windscreen is shattered, and I can make out two figures slumped in the front seats.

I park about twenty feet from the BMW, and get out. Time is tight. That patrol car can't be too far away now. I pull the camera out of its bag and take a wide shot. Head on, car with smashed windscreen. No bodies, just a good general shot to sell to any paper. Then I move in for the details.

Close-ups are harder to sell, but people want to see them. If they're strong, there's a market, if not in the press then on websites. I can see the driver is a male, slumped forwards like he's taking a nap at the wheel. The passenger is a girl, and she's fallen back and sideways onto him. There's a lot of blood. The engine is ticking over. That's strange, the old engine idling, as if they just pulled in to look at a map.

3

I'm still taking pictures, but I'm weighing it up. I was expecting a car smash, but this is more like a mafia hit. What comes to mind is those Sicilian pictures of a crusading mayor ambushed on his way to work, caught as he stumbled from the car, upper body in a dark pool on the road, feet still tangled in the pedals.

The boy has been shot through the neck, once at least. She's taken it in the chest, and her face is white except for a trace of blood around her lips. Maybe they tried to knock the gunman down? Or handbrake-turn the car and leave him standing? They must have tried something, since the engine was still running, but it hadn't worked.

I'm remembering the first book of photographs I ever saw. It was called 'The Rock n Roll Generation' - American kids in diners, at the drive-in, on the open road. There was one shot – through a windscreen – which was just like this scene. It showed a couple, parked up, and it looked like they were making up after a row. The guy was leaning forwards on the wheel, obviously upset, and the girl had her head on his shoulder, trying to explain it to him. Whatever it was.

It must be said, in photographic terms, this couple I'm framing make a fine picture. The dead do give great photographs. Pictures of the living look like frozen glimpses. Somehow, you feel you're not getting the full scene. The dead are different. Their silence fills the space inside a frame. These two were a picture waiting to be taken. As I take them, I can feel their shape - solid and exact – adding to the weight of the camera in my hand.

*

Imagine saying this to a child: "Doubt everything they tell you." Whoever *they* are. When I found a fossil snail in the quarry, I put it in my grandmother's hands. I was guessing at hundreds of millions of years. So many hundreds of millions that stone had

4

swallowed all the animals.

Her hands were like gloves – loose, thick and clumsy. She turned the fossil snail and then said "it's a fake." I told her I had cracked it from the rock myself. She handed it back to me, snail down, and went back to her pans of jam.

I'd like to think she was a literal believer in a seven-day creation. I'd like to say she sat me down with the Book of Genesis, and argued that God had laid the fossil record in the rocks to cover his creative tracks, or to give his children a sense of history. I'd like that, because then I could dismiss it.

In fact, there was no Bible in the house. No books at all. She didn't trust them. She believed nothing and no-one. "How do you know," she asked one morning over breakfast, "that I'm not poisoning you?"

So years later, when the police came to my door, wanting to comb my photographs for evidence, I said "How do you know I haven't doctored them?"

*

They can invent what they want. I'm not giving up my chemicals. Four baths. Developer first, the real magic. It still feels like I'm conjuring the images from nothing, out of blank sheets.

I get home and take the film out of the camera. Night is cooling so I close the windows, open curtains. I look out across the edgelands, and see blue lights heading for the warehouse yard, pointless sirens howling in the empty roads. I step into my darkroom, and begin my alchemy.

I drop a clean sheet in the first tray, and darkness bleeds into it, greys and blacks in the shape of a car. I work through the images - developing, stopping, fixing, washing - then I peg them to the drying racks.

They are great pictures, but when I get to the shots of the girl

I can't look. She upsets me. Maybe it's something about her face, but I've seen the faces of a thousand corpses. Whatever it is, it's physical. My guts make a fist and my heart jitters. I pull her out of the developer, and don't know what to do next. I can't bring myself to throw her pictures out, so I peg them up without putting them through the stop bath. That seems right somehow. Without the acid to arrest it, her image will bleed darker and darker until all the paper is black.

Usually by this stage I'd be on the phone to the picture desks, but this time I just leave them pegged out, and walk around the flat turning off all the radios.

I'm not thinking straight, and I've forgotten to clear up the darkroom. As I go back in I knock my thermometer off the wall. It breaks in half as it lands in the basin. Its silver spine smashes into beads like shot. I've never had to handle mercury, but I know it isn't good for you. I swill it down the sink, nudging it along with the side of my hand. Then I wipe my hand and worry that maybe I shouldn't have touched it at all.

It's not a good night. I feel I've lost some bearings. I sit in silence in a chair by the window. The edgelands are dark and still now. As my eyes adjust I can see across them, out into the fields of grain and rape beyond. In the middle of this prairie, I make out the distant wall of poplars which boxes in a tiny farmhouse, protecting it from gales, and from the vanishing horizons of its crops.

*

I'm driving back from the motorway. It's lunchtime. I'm keen to get home to develop my shots, and to eat. I see it from the car, and I slow down. I don't connect it with the A at that moment, but it does strike me as odd. I'm wondering if it's something to do with the murders. Everyone in town thinks Adam Sligo did it, and he's still on the loose, so it crosses my mind this might be his game.

I stop to take a picture. As I'm framing the shot, I see Petra Ware coming towards me. She's coming out of the edgelands, back towards town. I guess she's been to see the place where her son was killed. It's become a sort of shrine, so many flowers and toys and cards that the camping shop in town has put an awning over it, to keep the pilgrims dry.

I hear she goes there every day, and spends the rest of the time just walking. No-one knows if she's looking for the killer, or if she's just deranged with grief. She doesn't talk.

With this in mind I take my picture quickly, and turn to head back to my car.

"Wait," she calls. "I need a word with you."

I don't want to wait, but she knows I've heard her. She hasn't said a word to me since we left school, and she didn't say much to me then.

I say "Sorry about your son, Mrs Ware."

She nods. "There's a rumour you've got pictures of the murder."

"I've destroyed the film. Don't worry, you won't see anything in the papers."

She seems oblivious to my answers.

"Did they say anything to you?"

"No", I tell her. " It was over by the time I got there. I didn't know he was your son."

She keeps staring at me, as if she doesn't believe me, as if she's trying to force me to come out with it. I point at the B to explain what I'm doing, but she isn't interested.

In the car, I'm thinking about the B. It could have been coincidence, but it's the same red paint, a little neater than the A. It might have been a brush this time. I try to rationalise it as a game – Adam Sligo's game – so if the A was at the murder scene, the location of the B should be significant too. It's on a bus shelter, daubed across a poster of a woman running through the white surf on a beach. I think it's for perfume.

*

They say that by the time the police arrived at Petra Ware's front door, she knew her son was dead. The night of the murder was Marie's birthday. Her friends had planned a party, and Jake was in on it. Jake would pick her up from work in his car, then bring her to the Hunt Hotel bar where they would surprise her.

When Jake and Marie failed to show after an hour, some of their friends walked round to Mrs Ware's to see if there had been a mix-up. On the way, they saw the blue lights flashing past, heading for the edgelands. As soon as she saw who was at the door, she collapsed, blacked-out on her own front step. When she came round, she said "Jake's gone. There, I've said it." She had felt anxious for weeks, had sensed that some disaster was looming. The previous night she'd had a dream about her house, but the house was empty, no furniture, no family, just bare boards and walls, and the wind screaming through the glass-less windows.

So it was that the moment Jake's friends turned up to find him, long after he was due at the party, she knew. She knew there and then, and there was nothing his friends could say to talk her out of it.

The young policewoman sent to break the news found Petra in a trance, not interested in the news she had come to break. Within minutes of the WPC leaving, Jake's friends were naming Adam Sligo. His red pickup truck was seen heading for the edgelands earlier in the evening. TJ had seen him, because TJ lived just across the road from Sligo. It must have been him. TJ knew Sligo kept guns, and if anyone was enough of a psycho to use them on Jake and Marie, it was him.

8

Word got around very quickly. Jake and Marie were dead. Sligo was armed and missing. Within an hour, TJ and his brothers were on the roof of Sligo's bungalow. They had air rifles tucked under their arms, and stretched out between them was a huge banner saying LYNCH THE BASTARD. Down below, the rest of the kids were shouting support from the front lawn. Petra Ware got to hear about this and rushed down to stop them. She pleaded with them to let the police handle it, but in her heart she must have wanted Sligo dead.

Of course, neither he, nor his pickup ever came back to the house, but those kids stayed on the roof for hours. Even if Sligo was missing, they could still terrorise his old man. After all, he raised a killer. Petra didn't like that. She peered in through the net curtains, expecting to see Sligo's father cowering in a corner. Instead, she could just make out in the failing light a hunched and static figure in a chair, oblivious to everything, blankly watching TV with the volume on full. After seeing that, Petra started walking. She walked out to the edgelands to see where her son had died, then she walked back, and she's kept on walking, twelve to fifteen hours a day they say, in and out of the edgelands.

*

Adam Sligo was on the run for about a fortnight. Amazing really, because he never strayed more than a mile from the scene of his crime.

On the evening of the murders, he ran across the field behind the warehouses and dived into the Bluebird Centre, still open for late-night shopping. According to the newspapers, he spent the first few days and nights in there.

The rest of the story I got first-hand. Mister Motor is his trading name, a friend of mine. His business is in the edgelands, about half a mile from the Bluebird Centre. He divides his time

9

between clamping and crushing. His teams tow the clamped cars back to Mister Motor's yard, and he waits in his office, behind a metal grille. He does shifts, alternating with his wife. You can't blame him for sharing the burden. Everyone who visits him is livid, baying for blood.

So he's on duty one afternoon, and a man arrives in a pickup truck. He parks and walks into the office. He looks like a commando, full camouflage gear, and a gun rack on the back of his pickup. But his voice is quiet, and he isn't angry. He says he wants to buy a car.

Mister Motor clamps and crushes, but he doesn't sell. The commando says he doesn't want a car to drive, in fact he doesn't need an engine. He wants the shell of a car, and in particular he wants the shell of a blue car. Mister Motor tells him again that he doesn't sell, and he sends the man on his way.

Mister Motor doesn't see him for an hour or so, then notices, just as he's locking up the gates to go home, that the pickup is still there. Furious, he storms into the yard to get rid of this idiot. But there's no sign of the commando anywhere. That's worrying. Anything could happen in that yard, with wrecked cars piled up ten-high boot to bonnet.

Mister M calls, but no reply. He shouts and shouts, but no reply. He hears a sound, like a coughing or choking, and shouts again, but no reply. Much against his better judgement, but with no other options, he climbs into the piles of wrecks to see if he can find the man.

It's a difficult climb, into and out of broken, smashed up cars – in through the rear window, back seat, front seat, out through the windscreen. He's getting sliced and stabbed by the broken glass and metal. Finally he finds this man sitting in the driving seat of a written-off blue family saloon. His head is slumped over the wheel, and Mister Motor fears the worst, but when he reaches him the man is sobbing. His face is smeared with blood from the cuts on his hands. Mister M starts to give him a mouthful, but the man splutters something about his mum. This was his mum's car, he says. So Mister M – still fuming – tells him even if it was his mum's, it isn't now, because every car in the yard is waiting to be squashed into a tin-can. And besides, he says, this idiot is risking both their lives and breaking the law by being here.

The commando isn't making much sense, says he wants to buy the blue car. Mister M has lost it by now, screams out the facts again - the blue car's in a pile of cars ten-deep and isn't up for sale. He threatens to call the police if this lunatic doesn't get out of the car, and out of the yard, right now. The man doesn't move, and Mister M calls 999 on his mobile.

*

I was still a boy, about nine or ten, when I was sent to stay with my grandmother while my parents were splitting up. Of course, they didn't say that. They said they needed to redecorate the house, but I never saw the house again. Or my father.

Anyway, I was staying in the countryside, and I hated it. I hated my grandmother and her old, cold house. So one night I ran away. I took no food or drink, and had no plan or route in mind, so I only lasted one night.

When it was time to sleep that evening, I went into a copse at the side of the field, looking for a bush or something to hide under, and in the middle of the copse I found a car. It was an Austin Cambridge. A real car abandoned in the woods. The trees and bushes had grown around it, adopted it as one of their own. So it was almost completely camouflaged. The doors were rusted shut, but there was no windscreen, so I climbed in through the front. Once I'd jumped across into the back seat, I was in another world, a world of warm, dry leather, leaves and catkins. I felt completely safe, and I've never slept a better night than that. Ever

11

since, I've felt that cars were on my side.

Years later, I heard that Weejee made his car into a home. He furnished it with developing kit, spare flashbulbs, cameras, typewriter, clothes, salami and cigars. That Chevy Coupe was his bedroom, office, diner, darkroom.

So when I heard that Sligo ended up crying in the front seat of a car like his mum's, I felt quite close to him. Perhaps it was his mum's car? The papers would have looked into all that, if they'd known why he was in the car. But Mister Motor kept that to himself, and me. He told the police he thought Sligo was hiding. Just hiding.

By the time the police arrived at the yard, and Mister Motor pointed them towards the blue car's shell, Sligo had shot himself. That's the story. But I have a hunch that even if he'd run out of bullets, even if he didn't have a gun, the police may have helped him out.

*

It took me a couple of days to track Petra Ware down again. She was always walking, which made her difficult to trace. I found her at the end of an afternoon of solid rain. Driving back from a job, I saw her coming out of Sligo's bungalow. My first thought was that she'd killed the old man. All that walking, grieving, brooding, and still no explanation. Sligo had gone, without a trial, without any examination of motive, without remorse. The old boy was the only contact she had left with the man who killed her son. He was the only way of hitting back.

I offer her a lift, make some weak joke about the monsoon, and she climbs in beside me.

"Isn't that Sligo's house?"

"He hasn't a clue who I am, you know."

Afraid of the silence, I ask a few guarded questions and she tells me she's been shopping for the old man twice a week. She brings him food, cooks him a meal, discusses what's on TV. He never offers to pay, or thanks her for the food, but that makes it easier for her. If he knew who she was, if there was some emotional transaction between them, she would find that unbearable.

Despite TJ and his brothers climbing on the old man's roof, despite visits from the police and door-stepping reporters, he never mentions his son, and seems to know nothing at all about the murder. Petra has, she says, been making these visits from the week after it happened.

"Why do you do it for him?"

"It's not for him."

By now we're on the outskirts of town, heading for the edgelands. She sits forward in her seat, as if trying to read a distant road sign, then asks me to stop the car. She wants to get out. I tell her she'll be drenched, but she insists.

I pull up outside the Multiplex. There are teenagers – mostly around Jake's age – standing in the entrance, waiting for one film or another to begin. I wonder if Jake used to come here, and if that's why she wants to stop. There's a row of light-boxes by the swing doors, each with a posed still from a film in it. One's called 'The Distance', and the picture is a man running across a desert. He looks like he could run around the world and not be out of breath. She's about to shut the car door – without thanking me for the lift – when I reach across and hold it open.

"You asked me if Jake had said anything."

"You said no."

"I shouldn't have."

"What did he say?"

"She."

"What did she say?"

*

13

It's all too fragile. They found that out. Our lives are – my life was – built on nothing. Their deaths were built on nothing. That's what I was thinking, and I wanted to say it to her. I wanted to tell her to stop trying to understand what happened to her son. It was without meaning.

At first, I thought the alphabet appearing across the town might mean something, then Sligo died, and the letters kept coming. A motive from Sligo may have meant something. Locking him up, or lynching him may have meant something. But she didn't have any of that. She wanted some message from beyond the grave. I gave her one. Petra didn't want truth, she didn't want to know that when I reached the BMW they had both already crossed into silence.

It didn't matter what the message was, as long as it was unclear. I couldn't risk inventing a simple one, not knowing the details of their lives, their relationships. So I chose a single word and put it on the lips of Marie. I gave her the word SHANTY, and Petra took it in. For a moment, she looked quizzical, but not disappointed. I shrugged my shoulders, and she set off in the pouring rain to turn it in her mind. At last, she had a message, and the message was the meaning. She had something to work on – *Shanty. Shanty. Shanty. Shanty…*

Girl with Leaves in her Mouth
Jeanie O'Hare

"You're gorgeous, do you know that?"

He was surprised to hear himself say it. There had been a time when he could not bear to look at her, when her picture was in all the papers. Georgia slipped out of her coat and sat down. Richard was glad she was here but he wished he wasn't half-way through his lunch.

She pulled a supple, amber oak leaf from her mouth, unfurled it and placed it on the table. Richard took a look at it then looked at her. He touched the stem with his finger and aligned it with the cruet. He did not know what to say next. He had never expected to see her again. She looked calm. There was even a smile in her eyes.

The waiter was quite taken with her. He brushed the crumbs from the table, working sensitively around the leaf and laid a place setting for her. He offered to take her coat. Richard felt unable to speak whilst the waiter hovered. He felt unable to speak after the waiter had gone for more bread. Eventually he tried. "How are you?"

"Late it seems, judging by your plate."

He frowned. He knew immediately he was being teased. She carried on, "It's O.K. I won't mention the fact that you stood me up the last time we were supposed to meet. I just want to talk. Well . . . I want to hear you talk."

Richard had engineered this trip for himself. He was homesick.

There were a lot of old conversations he would be happy to have. And a few he would like to avoid. He could tell she was taking a good look at him while he re-filled his glass. He wondered if she found him older. He felt himself blush. He drained his glass of sparkling English mineral water and spoke quickly. "I don't really drink any more. Or come back here. My folks . . .are both dead. I go where I'm sent. I'm quite good at the rootless stuff. Loner. Self-sufficiency. You know?"

"No. Tell me."

He remembered he was not talking to a bored colleague. She brushed imaginary dandruff from her shoulder and found a small twig in her hand. She placed it beside the leaf.

"Green salad please."

The waiter was attentive. She placed her napkin on her lap, tipped the salad leaves onto the table in front of her and gave the plate back to him. He smiled, nodded and took it away. Richard looked down at his lamb with overworked mash. He had never taken much pleasure in his food. He cut the meat efficiently and moved it around in the puddle of mint sauce.

Georgia took a sprig of privet from her mouth, four or five small leaves on a long stem. She ran her tongue over her teeth and gave a little cough to make sure she had left none behind. She offered it to him but he would not join in with the joke. It fell to the floor a couple of feet from the table. They both watched it fall. On the carpet there were several other leaves, gathered near her chair, near her side of the table. She took another leaf, this time a dried, broken sycamore and blew it, like a kiss, from her outstretched palm. It floated gently onto his plate. His knife and fork clattered down.

"Don't be a bitch." He wondered if this trip had been such a good idea. He had not imagined getting angry with her.

He wanted it to be nice.

They went shopping. Town was an unimaginative mix of old and new. Flag stones clunked underfoot, concrete carparks slapped the sky ahead. They ignored the first few shops as they walked, then Georgia took the lead. He followed her into an accessory shop. "Let's buy sunglasses."

They tried on glasses for fun. She chose a retro pair. He was unimpressed.

"There is no British safety mark on them. They'll hurt your eyes." This statement alone persuaded her to buy them. He put his Rayban Aviator copies back in the exact place he had found them then tried to spin the rack. It stuck. She browsed through other things. There was not much for him to look at. Shopping together had always wound him up. He was always late for shopping trips.

She would end each Saturday by wagging her finger and explaining that it was unforgivable to be late.

He applied some lip salve from his own pocket and then felt like a shoplifter. He wondered where she was. At the desk the assistant was putting the sunglasses into a plastic box and putting the plastic box into a bag. She slid the assembly across the counter with a smile. Georgia took a crisp oak leaf from her mouth, smoothed it out, apologised for having nothing smaller and gave it to the shop girl. She snapped back the clip on the notes drawer, put the leaf in the till, and counted out the change to Georgia. She pushed the till drawer shut with her hip and switched her attention to the next person in the small queue.

On the street Georgia left the glasses in her pocket. They both took silent note of the cloudless sky. He knew she would not wear them, she probably didn't even like them. Irritation flickered through him. Now he recognised her. There she was, stranded in some small way by spite, waiting for him to rescue her. He didn't want to. She spoke anyway. "It was cold waiting on that bench. Should I have known you weren't going to come?"

To get to the park they would take a bus. Richard paid the fares and let Georgia choose the seats. He followed her unsteadily up the stairs to the back of the empty top deck. He heard himself 'tut'. They would barely have taken their seats when it would be time to get off. Georgia sat in the corner of the back seat. Richard sat next to her, but not too near. He found himself staring down the aisle towards the front of the bus, uncomfortably aware of anyone who might emerge from the stairwell.

The road swept down the hill and straight through the heart of the town. The park lay undisturbed and waiting a mile or so away. Richard groaned as the bus turned off the main road. This was a 24, it would go meandering through the estates to the school.

"We're going to the hell-hole. Hold tight." She touched his arm. He felt a little sick.

The bus swung into the slip road by the school. The weight of bodies pouring onto the rocking bus added to his nausea. 'Lazy gits' he thought, most of them are only going half a mile. This had been his bus, hers too. Maybe that's why she chose the back seat.

The bus started moving again. A group of gangly, animated boys each sporting their own experiment with facial hair, made their way casually towards Richard and Georgia to claim the back seat. The five boys stood twitching, chewing and waiting to sit down. They slouched at angles watching the couple. The gawkiest boy dragged his sweaty palms along the metal ceiling of the bus. It made a loud squeaking noise. Richard thought he should speak. For the first time he noticed there was a leaf on each of the surrounding tartan cushions. The boy with curly hair looked at Georgia who motioned with her hand to one of the empty seats. He picked up the leaf very gently and sat with it on his lap. The other four boys sat where they were invited to and did the same. They sat looking from her to him and back again but saying nothing. Richard wondered if they recognised her.

Without warning Georgia put her hand behind Richard's neck and pulled him towards her. She began to kiss him. The boys watched. Richard closed his eyes. Self-conscious panic took hold of him. The kiss seemed endless. He broke away, staring ahead, straight down the aisle through the window to the horizon. He felt stupid. Georgia gave a little giggle. Richard looked immediately at the boy with curly hair who was fixed by Georgia's gaze. On his lap there was now a pile of leaves. Richard looked at the other four boys; each of them sat silently, perfectly still, with a small pile of leaves on their laps, their hands sorting through them gently. The bus went over a pothole. Some leaves fell to the floor. The curly headed boy looked anxious, apologetic. Georgia smiled and shook her head. She ran her hand through her hair and produced a beautiful, pale green chestnut leaf and presented it to his bashfully outstretched hand. He blushed.

Richard's nausea returned. He was aware of cold saliva around his lips. He wanted to get off the bus. They all sat there, in silence, for the rest of the journey, swaying in unison around corners and nodding together at junctions.

The boys were waist deep in leaves by the time Georgia took Richard's hand and insisted, "This is our stop." They were three stops short of the park. She glided downstairs. He stumbled after her, leaves stuck to the soles of his shoes. The bus pulled up at the market square with an animal-hiss of its brakes.

Richard was panicked by the bus journey. He didn't know what he wanted out of this day anymore. It wasn't what he had expected. He sat on the low wall by the florists. When he looked up he could see the sixth formers pressing themselves against the window as the bus pulled off. They weren't looking at him. He looked around for Georgia.

"Let's not go down there."

But she was way ahead of him. He followed her down the side road past the back of the police station to the dog pound. This was a route to the park he would never have taken. He knew a thousand routes around town and none of them took him anywhere near here. He scanned the carpark full of stolen cars.

"Please, Georgia, c'mon."

She stopped right where he knew she would. The dogs were in day pens. In the last cage were two dogs together, an older shaggy one and a young aggressive thing. She turned to Richard to make sure she had his attention.

She had once been afraid of dogs.

She offered her sleeve through the bars. The oldest dog came forward and sniffed her hand. The other dog licked her fingers. She opened her palm. Richard watched her closely. He loved watching her but he was shocked to see her hands so dirty. She turned her hand over. There was soil in the lines around her knuckles and mud under her nails. Before he could say anything the older dog pushed its long snout through the bars and began truffling under her skirt. She carried on stroking the dog's head. It knew her. It found its way under the fabric of her skirt then suddenly pulled back. Richard had never seen a dog walk backwards before. All barking stopped. Both dogs retreated and sat against the far wall of the pen. Richard took Georgia's hands and looked at them. She pulled away from him.

He wanted desperately to hold her.

When he caught up with her she had reached the park and stood holding the railings staring across to the ponds. Children in bright colours were playing noiseless games with frisbees and kites on the lush green hillside. The breeze took their voices away. A small white dog ran in a straight line between two people, one at the top of the hill, one at the bottom. It all looked innocent. Nearest to the gate two seven year old footballers with no other team-mates to evade were shouting "man on! man on!"

She turned to him. "Let's go back."

"But you used to love it. . ." He cut off. He had said something stupid. He was feeling awkward in her company again. He glanced at her then looked at the ground. She was waiting for him, somehow unable to cross the gravel at the gate, unable to enter the park. She was waiting for him to comfort her. Like she always did.

He watched himself kick over some stones trying to stay calm. He was not sure what he was feeling now. He was having a rush. He realised he felt high, bright with some sort of expectation. Could it be joy? She was looking across the park to the ponds. He looked at her shoulder, at her bruised neck. He asked himself if her still loved her. He thought maybe he should hold her. Maybe then he would know.

He kissed the top of her head, breathing in the scent from her hair. He wrapped his body around her. She felt cold. It scared him. He could feel his heart beat. A dampness invaded his nostrils. He wanted to pull out of the embrace but he was too scared to look at her face, his old fear returning. There had been a time when he couldn't stand to look at her. He held his breath. He didn't want to breathe her in any more. She didn't smell like she used to. She smelt of leaves and grass, of leafmould and earth.

He closed his eyes then eased back, his hands holding her shoulders. He looked at her. That wasn't calm in her eyes, it was something duller. He needed her to speak.

She did. She said what he needed to hear.

"We did have a good time in there didn't we?" He nodded but he could not follow it up with a smile. He felt too full of emotion. He let his hands drop. He was glad to let go of her. He looked across the park. They did have some fantastic times in there, meeting, after dark, on their bench.

But then love gave way to irritation. And the last time he hadn't shown up.

She had spent a whole night in there once, lying perfectly still, twisted a little into the ground, leaves in her open mouth, waiting for some dog walker to find her in the morning.

He suggested a swim. Swimming had always been a hit with Georgia. It was a swimming and shopping town, no cinema. Georgia excelled at both.

She wore a red two-piece and swam teasingly around him in circles as he crawled back and forth. The pool was quiet and all the attendants looked bored. They stood in small groups chatting. One of them used a net to scoop a single cigarette butt out of the water. Richard reached the shallow end and stopped for breath. Behind him, floating in lazy arcs on the surface of the water were perhaps forty or fifty leaves. Closest to him two blackened acorns spun manically on the tiny whirlpools which caught up with him as he stopped. He watched them sink.

He hooked his arms around the rail near the metal steps, lay back and let his legs float up. He looked at her body. Her skin was refracted white under the surface. She looked young, hardly more than fifteen. He tried not to look at the dirt streams running down from her nose. She would hit him later for not telling her. He wanted to touch her. She doggy-paddled for a while then rested her feet on the bottom. A film of dust rested on the surface of the water around her shoulders. She studied her water puckered hands and complained that chlorine made her teeth feel rough. She reached into her mouth with wet fingers and pulled out another oak leaf to float on the surface of the pool. He'd had enough.

He dived away from her. This time though it was difficult to get any real speed going. His limbs felt heavy. Maybe it was the lunch sitting in his stomach. One or two leaves touched his lips. He spluttered. He dipped his face in the water. When he resurfaced one small leaf clung to the side of his face like a birthmark. He swam on. The deep end of the pool seemed a long way off. He would do four more lengths then call it a day.

As he turned and kicked at the wall he looked up for her. She was under the water. He knew she was going to jump up at him. The attendants were on their break. There were leaves everywhere. He was not going to indulge her any longer. He swam back towards the shallow end.

He grew impatient. He stood up, leaves clinging to his thighs and trunks. He looked around for her. She was taking full advantage of the attendants' absence. He dipped below the water and began looking for her.

He could not see her. It was darker now, the leaves filtered the light. He pushed his limbs through the water going beyond the shelf at the shallow end, down the slope towards the centre of the pool. Up above his head the entire surface was now covered in leaves. Even the gap where he had stood was now slowly closing up. The covering of the pool was complete. Except, he thought he saw light flickering through, over there. He thought he saw Georgia swim through a column of dim light. The water grew darker still. It seemed dirty. His feet left the bottom. He reached out to the side towards the rail. He was further from the edge than he thought. He panicked. Where were the vents and the rails? He couldn't make out the pattern of the tiles anymore. He couldn't gauge how far the surface was. He tried to swim. His clothes were soaked and heavy. He swam then stopped. He was caught on something. He wrestled with his coat. His lungs were hurting. He had to make a decision. He couldn't see. He had to stop panicking.

He would trust the water. If he kept still it would take him up. He would be safe. Georgia would save him. He let his body go. He let the water take him. He called out for her. Bubbles broke through the pondweed on the surface. She would have to forgive him now. He too would have his picture in the paper.

The Golden Boys
Gerard Woodward

I'd just arrived for my interview for the position of
manager at Rabbit & Pumpkin – London's largest children's
bookshop, when I was suddenly struck by the odd and rather
alarming fact that I hadn't passed water for two days.

In every other respect my preparation had been
meticulous, I'd thoroughly researched the company, (a subsidiary,
I was interested to learn, of the American entertainment
conglomerate *Etna*, which also ran a chain of bookmakers and
whose philosophy was summarised in its tag line - *Spend to Play,
Play to Spend*), I'd picked the children's buyer's brains at the regular
bookshop where I was currently deputy manager for what was hot
in tot and teenage literature at the moment, and I'd reread the
management training handouts I'd accumulated in attending
countless courses. Sartorially I thought I had got it just right –
smart but informal, colourful yet sober, wild yet neatly pressed.

But all morning I was bothered by the feeling that I'd
overlooked some crucial detail. I felt as if I was at the airport
without my passport, or had just finished a huge and expensive
meal at a select restaurant only to notice the emptiness of the
pocket where my wallet should have been. And it was then as I
strolled into Rabbit & Pumpkin itself, that I realised my visits to
the bathroom for the last two days had been purely ablutionary,
that I had used the lavatory only in its literal sense, as a place to
wash.

It wasn't as if I hadn't been taking in water. Fluids had entered my body at their usual rate, of that I was sure, but somehow they'd managed to stay there, or else by some mysterious metabolic process, had evaporated. It was rather like being told of the death of an old friend you hadn't seen for years and had all but forgotten about. It is only when they die that you remember them. I suddenly felt nostalgia for a bodily process. I missed that morning fall and splash. And then I panicked, imagining myself caught short during my interview, as surely the build up of water in my bladder must any moment tip over and weigh its accumulated volume for release.

But even as I browsed the three gleaming floors of Rabbit & Pumpkin I felt no need to go. I forgot about my unusual condition as I took in the ambience of the store. Apart from the contents of the shelves and a purple rocking horse, grotesquely huge with pink spots that occupied the entrance area of the ground floor, there was little to indicate that this shop had anything to do with childhood. In fact it struck me as a building designed to baffle, trap and even hurt children, rather than educate and entertain them. The shelves were of smoked glass, the floors mirror-smooth marble, the stairs of the same stone, each edge razor-sharp, banistered with hi-tension cables. Security guards in black neo-fascist garb stalked the floors.

I remembered reading somewhere about the philosophy underlying this hard-edged Spartan design. It was meant to echo the purity of childhood. *'Our stores have the freshness of little children, unblemished of soul or body...'*

My interview was with three men – Bob, the manager whom I hoped to replace, Tim the assistant manager and Mike, the pre-school buyer. The interview was conducted in a cramped little room that housed assorted junk – piles of books were stacked everywhere like termite mounds, there were some big promotional cartoon cut-outs of Mr Toad and Mr Badger, and a bank of tv monitors occupied the two walls behind my interviewers. I found these monitors very distracting. They offered a seemingly limitless number of perspectives on the shop, each one flicking automatically to a different camera every few seconds, a caption identifying the locale (*rear entrance, teenage fiction, Pooh Corner*). Each time I was asked a question I found my attention drifting towards these screens, noticing how still people became in bookshops, just standing there, browsing.

I was invited to remove my jacket. I declined, remarking that I wasn't hot. I then noticed that my three interviewers were all shirtsleeved. And when later in the interview Tim informed me that Rabbit & Pumpkin was very much a 'hands on, jackets off' kind of company, I realised I had stumbled at the very first fence.

"Do you have children yourself?" asked Mike, a man whose prematurely bald scalp was as waxed and polished as a showroom car's.

"I'm afraid not," I replied slowly, wondering if they had the right to ask that question. My slowness came across as guilt.

"Not a problem," said Tim, the youngest and plumpest of the three, "neither do we."

The trio gave synchronised chuckles.

" 'I'm afraid not,' you say", Bob said, "but the truth is we find blokes with young families…" he paused, looked past me, looked at me, looked past me, "…they can get into difficulties working for a company like Rabbit & Pumpkin."

"It's the hours," said Mike, "we had a guy here, he used to…" Mike began sniggering violently into his notes, shaking his head, "he used to cry, do you remember, Bob…"

"Yes," said Bob smiling fondly

"…he used to go on about how he missed his little daughter…" Mike tried holding tears of laughter back by a finger and thumb pressed to his eyes.

"If your tombstone had room for only one word apart from you name etcetera, what word would that be?"

Tim, who'd asked this question with a stern face, crossed his legs twice, three times, settled his notebook on his knee, held a pen poised to record my response.

I looked passed him at a monitor and saw a woman in *Enid Blyton* slip a paperback into her coat.

I struggled to find a word. I had not expected to encounter my own grave in a children's bookshop. I could see it but its marble face was blank. A stream of words was swiftly chiselled into it but they seemed nonsensical – *cheese; corrugated; ice; heirophantically*. I could sense tall Bob, the one in the middle, smirking as I struggled to pick one. Eventually a useable word appeared.

"Honesty," I said, then "Truth".

The trio nodded with thoughtful approval.

"Honesty extending to matters concerning the ownership of objects?" said Bob, his eyes meeting mine only for a second.

Of the three it was Bob I found most unsettling. Not only did he refuse to meet my eye from behind his wire-framed spectacles, but he wore a permanent and ambiguous smile. The long length of his body was folded succinctly into his chair. His complexion was ruddy, smooth, blossom-soft. His hair was roughly-cut, brass-coloured curls. His lips pouted grotesquely when he spoke. He seemed to sip his sentences before producing them. Most irritatingly he had a tendency to begin his sentences with the stub-ends of mine.

"I'm not sure what you mean."

"What I mean is personal integrity and security. Once or twice we've found a creature amongst us…it's an unpleasant path to go down. Money was disappearing from some of the tills. Now there are all sorts of things one can do, miniature cameras, money that leaves traces on the hands, all sorts of horrible things…. And she was such a charming girl, the last person we suspected. She had some sort of habit to feed. She was led out in handcuffs and said tearful goodbyes to the colleagues she'd tried to frame for her thieving. We don't want a creature like that working here again…"

He tasted his lips, smiled.

"I'm not a creature like that," I said and noticed a flicker of irritation cross Bob's roseate face as I unconsciously borrowed his sentence-borrowing habit.

"Your greatest failure?" Said Mike briskly as if ticking through a checklist.

"My marriage," I replied.

"Honesty," whispered Bob to himself.

"All your fault?" Said Tim, smiling.

"I wouldn't see that exactly…"

"Another man?" Said Mike lifting his eyes from his pad for the first time in ages.

"No…"

"Another woman?"

"It's confusing isn't it, relationships and all that," said Mike to Tim, then to me, "did you ask her if she knew how to ride a bike?"

"I'm not entirely comfortable with this line of questioning, if you don't mind," I said, flushing.

"Absolutely," said Tim, suddenly looking worried, "it's just that none of us three are married," he waved his biro at the other two, "you know, so its interesting for us to hear…" His sentence petered out. Bob rekindled it,

"To hear about life in the world beyond bachelerdom," he said. "You know, the worst thing about it was how she tried to pin the blame on her friends. She would come up to me and suggest I kept an eye on so and so, in the end you just didn't know who to trust. Well," a quick double look at his two companions, "interview over, I think."

Closing rituals were observed, hands shaken, pleasantries exchanged, exits made. Further interviews were being held the following week. I wouldn't hear before then. Just as I was leaving a sphincter somewhere deep in my body opened and a cascade of water tumbled through me, halting only at the last, tiny round muscle before the outside world.

The company loo was as shiny and spotless as the shop floor. There were three stalls. I stood at the central one, unzipped, produced myself and waited. I heard the door behind me open and two men enter. As usually happens on these occasions another door deep in my bowels slammed shut and I couldn't go. I had hoped that the weight of accumulated wee would have been great enough to overcome this annoying shyness, but evidently it wasn't. I stood there dry and mute as the two men flanked me, produced their members and peed with gusto. I sensed, out of the corner of both eyes, these two plump, pink lengths of flesh held with the tenderness of surgeons. To my right the more powerful flow gave a sound of cup after cup of bone china being hurled at a wall. To my left the stream came out at a steep fall and in pulses that quickly drained. Thin clouds of steam rose. I was the dry channel between these copious canals, having given up any hope of breaking the ramparts that now held my water supply. I'd left it too long to pretend I'd just finished (a quick mime of a shake) and too long to be waiting for the commencement. I was just standing there not going, my penis an unproductive lump in my fingers. Those few centimetres of nakedness seemed to unclothe me entirely. I had no option but to stand it out, huddle myself in a cocoon of personal space, hood myself in phallic self-contemplation and wait for my neighbouring floods to withdraw. I'd invested too much of myself at this central stall to leave it now. (At my foot was the trough drain, gargling on lemony rivers from both directions at once.)

34

It seemed an hour had passed before the man on my left gave his last pulse of pee, let a dozen or so drips fall, pummelled his piece with a technique I was unable to observe in detail, tucked himself away and zipped up. As he turned to leave I sensed him pause and look at me. I glimpsed the bland, smooth cranium of Mike. He hesitated, as if about to say something, and then left.

I was rocking back and forth on my heels as the flow to my right finished. I sensed this man too turn towards me. I then glimpsed the awful fact that he was holding out his hand towards me. I stole a shy glance to my right. It was tall Bob, the curly-haired, rosy-faced manager.

I folded my unused self away and reluctantly put my hand in his. He shook it firmly.

"You don't remember me do you?" He said. He held on to my hand for as long as it was seemly to do so.

"You're the person who interviewed me just now."

He laughed, revealing a new, complicated face.

"No, not just now, I mean from before then. From way back…" He said this as he walked towards the loo door. He was leaving without washing his hands. Since our conversation had become ambulatory I felt obliged to follow him out of the toilets and onto the shop floor, also without washing my hands.

"I'm sorry, I'm not sure I remember…"

During the interview Bob had seemed silent, quiet, uninspiring, but in motion, able to use and demonstrate his height he gained a stature and authority that unsettled me. I felt like a page carrying a king's train.

"St Nicola's," he said over his shoulder, smiling at a customer, then turned to me, "they called us The Golden Boys, you and me. We were five or six. The Golden Boys…"

But a customer with a complicated enquiry about a pop-up book intervened and Bob began a hunt for this book which I was unwilling to follow. I didn't speak to him again and left the shop puzzled, wondering if some coded signal of approval had been given, that I'd got the job. Or perhaps it meant the opposite.

How was I to interpret Bob's claim of childhood friendship? He did not dwell in any alcove of my memory. I felt certain of this. But then neither did much else from those times. It worried me. When I thought back to my first years at primary school it was like walking around the shop after closing. Everything was in place, the rooms were in the right order, the furniture was where it should be, but there were no people, or if they were they were like mannequins, their faces standardised childhood faces – freckled, odd-toothed, tousle-haired. The longer I thought about them the less defined they became, their features disappearing altogether, leaving bland, smooth membranes. There were Christian names, the huge faces of teachers, wooden clocks, buckets of grey plasticine, blunt cutlery and scissors, the odour of simmering tureens. But somewhere in the intervening thirty years I had carelessly let the identities of my infant companions slip into a convenient abyss. I felt anger at my carelessness, to have not retained that information. And so much of what I am today could have been moulded back then. Bob, who claimed a significant stake in those years, what gestures, linguistic tics, opinions and ideas that I now think of as essentially me might he have endowed me with during those years in which we maybe played marbles on sunlit drain covers endlessly?

I began to feel that the abyss down which those childhood memories had been tipped was the same one that now provided a bottomless reservoir for my water. There was a deep chasm somewhere down there which I could neither fill nor draw from.

More waterless, unflowing days passed. The whole rhythm of things had gone, yet I felt a lightness and energy I hadn't felt in years. It was this that prevented me from visiting my doctor. I felt vigorous, alert, clean and dainty. How could I call on my GP feeling so well? But there was something out of kilter. It was as though the daily flow of water from my body had measured some essential cycle in me, the daily filling and emptying of my cistern, that once switched off kicked my life out of synch with itself.

A childhood memory did come to me during those days, but it was a later one. Staying with an uncle in a tiny Welsh village for two weeks. He had an outside loo that was alive with spiders, snails and woodlice. For the whole two weeks I didn't defecate once. I was amazed by my body's ability to retain its products, and when I returned home I endured an hour of grinding agony on our own plush toilet. I had always been conscious, during those two weeks, of the geological build-up in my bowels, the sedimentary strata slowly hardening, petrifying. And I knew that I was in for a difficult time when it came to removing them. It wasn't as though my solid waste had simply disappeared. I was not conscious now of carrying around a week's build-up of water inside me, sloshing like a loaded petrol can. It just wasn't there. The twisted loops of my guts had a kink in them somewhere down which my liquid intake was vanishing.

There was an odd smell on my right hand that I couldn't wash off. A smell of fresh bread, warm yeast, wet seaweed.

Nearly a week had passed since my interview. I'd been working late at the shop on an author-event and had stayed for a few drinks at The Unicorn before taking the tube home.

Near the tube station is Tim's Kebab, a Formica emporium of skewered lamb, rum babas and rotating meat loaf at which I would often stop to satisfy a hunger pain after a late night. I purchased a special doner, a pitta envelope stuffed with reams and ribbons of thin meat like a letter from an over-friendly pen pal. I gnawed at this warm bundle as I walked the empty lime avenues that connected my first floor flat with the underground station.

There was Bob walking towards me.

"Final interviews tomorrow," he said, unsurprised to see me. Somehow I felt unsurprised at seeing him. He was starting to look familiar.

"Great," I said. I had already decided I didn't want to work for Rabbit & Pumpkin.

"You should hear from us by the end of the week. That looks nice, where did you get it?"

"Tim's Kebab," I said, swallowing underchewed doner, "near the tube."

"Really? I've never tried it. Lived here all my life. Mind you, I'm not that keen on kebabs," he chuckled wetly, "anyway, see you."

"Yes, see you."

When I got home I found a little stalactite of cold, opaque fat hanging from the heel of my hand.

On Friday I received a letter from Rabbit & Pumpkin. It was hand-written in watery brown ink. It came straight out with it -

"After careful consideration we have decided not to offer you the post of manager at Rabbit & Pumpkin.

Our decision was a difficult one. In the end we felt that your personality lacked a certain quality we call 'knowing naivety'. We also sensed that you were uncomfortable with your age. You kept referring to your childhood as 'many moons ago', for instance, which only served to make you seem older than you actually are.

I hope you are not too disappointed. As a mark of gratitude for your taking an interest in us I am enclosing a complimentary copy of a book that is doing rather well in the tots section.

Yours sincerely
Bob

The book was a thick board book called Raymond the Rainbow, a peculiar tome telling the story of a day in the life of a meteorological phenomenon. There was Raymond, all seven colours of him, sitting at his table having breakfast, Raymond going for a walk in the countryside, meeting his friends Sammy Sun and Ronald Rain; Raymond doing his tough day's work of being a rainbow; Raymond doing the gardening, watching telly, brushing his teeth, going to bed. Is there something missing from that list of activities? Yes, of course, the activity that is missing from all children's books.

A few nights later I was walking towards Tim's Kebab from home when I met Bob coming the other way with a wad of pitta and meat attached to his face.

"I thought you didn't like kebabs."

"You were enjoying yours so much I thought I'd try one. Rather nice…" He gasped the words between difficult swallows. Chilli sauce was smeared around his mouth like clumsily applied lipstick, "listen, I hope you're not too upset about the job…"

I closed my eyes in a dismissive gesture as if to say it was the least of my problems. Bob laughed, picked out a strip of meat and fed it to the red fish that was his mouth.

"Of course, it had nothing to do with your failure to recall our early life together. I hope you don't think that…you still haven't remembered have you?"

I shook my head.

"I thought you might have remembered by now. We were best friends. We were famous throughout St Nicola's for our peeing games. We had contests among the trees in the corner of the playground, side by side, arches of pee – who could send it furthest? You always won. We'd rotate like lawn sprinklers," here he performed an illustrative mime, the kebab serving as a penis, "spray our audiences. They'd laugh. We'd cross piss swords, duel with them. You could pee so high and far the sunlight caught in its spray and made tiny rainbows. You were the boy who could piss rainbows. I thought Raymond the Rainbow might remind you. And the letter I wrote. It was in my own urine, mixed with ink. Thought it might trigger something. I was always envious of your superior jet, the way you made your pee fly. You sent yourself into the clouds. I was Robin to your Batman…" He paused, looked at his kebab as if it had suddenly transformed into a living thing and dropped it. "Do you remember now?"

I didn't say anything as he took a handkerchief from his pocket, wiped his mouth and hands…

"I don't like kebabs," he said, looking down at the burst pita on the pavement, "I've never liked them."

I must have walked the lime avenues between Tim's Kebab and my flat several thousand times but that night I briefly became lost. It was midsummer and the trunks of the lime trees had bushed out, almost blocking the pavements in places. I found myself wandering in a maze of them in roads whose names I didn't recognise. I found my way home only by chance.

This was two years ago. I haven't seen Bob since. Nor have I passed water.

I find myself bothered increasingly by trivial questions which I have to write down in a notebook in the hope that I'll be able to answer them one day. Here are just a few (I've numbered them)

47 – how did the fish get to be in a mountain lake two thousand feet up a mountain in Wales? Did they swim up from sea level?

279 - What is the earliest surviving example of initials carved in a tree?

438 – The noise made by pelican crossings – where does

it come from? The lights? The push-button box, or somewhere else? You can't tell by listening (presumably because there is a stereophonic effect.)

As for my past, I have lost all interest in it. In fact, I genuinely feel I have no past. The present covers a period of the last three or four years, beyond that there is nothing. And the space of the present is shrinking. The puddle of my nowness is evaporating. Except for this smell I have on my right hand. It reminds me of something from way back. Biscuits, perhaps, from the oven in my mother's house. Or from the bark that was up to my nose when I climbed a tree in her garden. Something like that.

Pictures From A Wide Wet World
Amanda Dalton

In her bathroom Alice has a painting of a woman with a blue
yacht balanced on her head. Or rather, had a painting. Had.

Yesterday she'd filled the bath as usual, got in, washed a bit – a
vague wash, running almost out of steam before she'd started.
Then she'd lain there in a wettish torpor, neck cricked on the
bath-edge, and she'd stared for an age at the painting on the wall.

Until it had quite suddenly become too much for her: being in the
water, wet and tired, and the love of her life in Holland, maybe,
and being thirty eight but feeling eighty three, and all alone, and
that woman up to her waist in cold sea with a heavy wooden boat
on her poor head. *Think of the splinters*, Alice had thought. Then,
*Think of your skull nearly breaking; your neck in spasm, your knees shaking
underneath that weight.* And worse still, *Think of sinking under, drowning
in the grey sea, all because of balancing a boat on your poor head.*

Alice had shuddered then, and slid a bit and splashed as she'd
risen up, Goddess of the Seaweed, full of wrath and righteous
indignation. *What will the people see?* she had thought. *The people on
the bank or the beach? They'll see a lovely blue yacht, bobbing on the waves,
and they'll have no idea of the woman underneath it, buckled, drowning in the
dark, the bottom of the boat a coffin lid shut down on her already.* And with
a cleaning windows kind of skid and squeak, Alice had lunged at

the painting, snatched it from its hook and thrown it down. The glass had cracked, the painting skewed in its frame.

It had left a grey dust oblong on the wall. *Filthy,* she would have thought if she had been feeling quite herself.

She had touched her own head then. Standing still in the bath and dripping a little, she had put her fingers to her scalp, with caution, as if it might be bruised or dented, or as if she might discover there a ridge of wood, a keel, the beginnings of the hull and rudder jutting through her hair. And she had cried a bit, mainly for the woman in the painting who must ache, who must be desperate, who must be about to drown.

That was yesterday.

Of course, she'd stepped out of the bath eventually, dried off, dabbed at her wet eyes, dressed. She hadn't really cried, not enough to blow her nose; little enough, in fact, to pretend it never was – just a tear or two that mingled with the general damp and drips. Alice only ever cried in the bath, and for that reason. She hated to think of herself as a cryer and this way she needn't. Though once, the crying in the bath thing had got out of hand. When she was twelve, her Uncle Sammy emigrated to Australia and she had worked so hard at not crying that she'd strained her throat and her neck glands all swelled up and she couldn't speak for days. Then she'd got in the bath and out the blue had cried and cried, real shakes and blubbers, like an awful storm at sea. She was terrified. She kept splashing her hands in the water so no-one would hear the gusts of sobbing. When they eventually calmed a bit she got out and dabbed at her face along with the rest of the drying, but she was so upset and shaken she forgot herself and blew and blew her nose into the towel. Great big blows, all elastic sticky and unspeakably, shamefully, vile. She'd tried to wash it off in the bath, fast, before the water all swirled down the hole, and then she'd had to pretend the towel had accidentally fallen in. And, of course, her mum never said a word, but Alice knew damn well she'd handed her a bath towel full of snot and, worse still, she'd been caught out telling lies.

Oh Alice.

*

Today some post has come from Holland. Alice has put it on the worktop in the kitchen while she peels potatoes. Not that she's casual; she's read it seven times. It's a photograph, in black and white. Punts on a river, anchored, 'put in' at a jetty; the water's dull and creased, like corrugated steel. A man, who is little more than a grey blur, sits on the far boat. He might be waving, or he might be pulling down his hat, shading his eyes in a bright light. The other men lie flat across their boats, as if they're sleeping. On the back it's stamped and addressed just like a postcard, and there's a message: *Alice - I'm the one awake, but only just. Making a little money doing this. For now. As always. Max. x*

Now she's ignoring it, while she gets on with potatoes, glancing through her kitchen window at the yard she sometimes dignifies by calling 'patio', or even 'terrace'. Below it, there's a proper garden – proper, but invisible from here. Here it's all grey: weather, slabs and gravel, and the puffed-up pigeons that keep coming back because of Mr Hargreaves feeding everything that lives (except for slugs, which he collects and puts next door – the other way). Here, it's grey as Max's photograph.

Alice drags her fingertips along the bottom of the bowl, through potato soil and grit. She thinks she feels the give of silt and mud along a river bed, and fancies that her index fingers might become the poles to push potato-punts. Her little fingers splash like arms draped at the boat's edge, drifting, and the water's turning brownish as she floats, a scud that breaks the surface.

Plop. She drops another potato bomb from the sky. It splashes the post. Alice glances down at the watery brown smear settling on the gloss of photograph. It doesn't bother her. She has a headache, sharp along her skull like a wound, *from stem to stern,* she thinks, and touches it. Ouch. She wonders if she has some psychic power: the boat painting, those unexpected tears, her outrage in the bath. She'd thought that Max was packing and unpacking soldier's kit bags. In a warehouse. And she'd thought that he'd be gone for ten or twelve weeks at the most. She'd thought.

She wipes her hands and then the photograph across her jeans, puts it closer to her face, as if her eyesight's failing, or as if she's sniffing for a hidden clue. Her face is ancient, like a map with every contour marked, a line for every journey she might make, for every waterway to Max, every dead end. *Who took this photograph?* And whether she asks in her head, or in a whisper, or right out loud, Alice doesn't have the first idea.

*

"He'll turn up out the blue, you'll see."
"I thought you were over him"
"You're worth better."
"Bastard"
"This postcard thing's just weird."

"It isn't weird. He's playing games."

"You mustn't have him back"

"Alice" – This is Maddy, down from the bathroom – "Where's that painting gone? The one with the woman in the water with a big boat on her head?"

Alice's friends are fuelled with the heat of female solidarity, and wine, and sausages and mashed potatoes – mountains of them. Alice's comfort food. Alice is feeling strange. She hadn't meant to say a word about the postcard. Better to let it rest – Max in Holland, maybe. Probably forever. (Always was a wanderer, a flaky geezer; jobs abroad are just the coward's way of saying goodbye). They have no idea how much she misses him, longs for him, and it's best that way. *Longing is potentially embarrassing, like crying,* thinks Alice.

But at the table she had drifted off again, forgotten how to smile and speak and listen, found herself creating gravy lakes and rivers, thin canals with mashed potato tow paths. Her sausages had almost floated. They were heavy-duty punts, the kind that she imagined would be used to transport cargo, and they were a pig to steer.

She'd looked up from her plate, just for a second, just to add a little extra gravy, and she'd caught a whiff of anxious silence in the air. Her friends were staring, all except for Jude, whose eyes were wandering around the mustard jar, a little wild. With the smallest sigh, Alice spoke: "I've had a sort of postcard. It's from Max."

And now they won't shut up with their advice, except for Caro, who is drunk and slightly mad (and shouldn't be in charge of the infants, which she is, along with Alice - strewth.). She's demonstrating how to make an origami boat. She's going to sink it in a bowl of water, yet it will remain completely dry. No one cares, remotely, except Alice, who'll be interested in anything that takes attention from her, interested in how to make a guilloche, even. So she nods at Caro and she says "Go on. Go on, I'm listening," while the others talk amongst themselves, about betrayal, men and unrequited love and photographs; while Alice swallows down what starts to feel like motion sickness or perhaps a flapping fish that's trapped inside her tubes.

*

A guilloche is an ornamental border or a moulding formed of interlacing bands enclosing roundels. Alice's father used to talk about such things at home. She doesn't have a clue why she remembered it just now. She's standing in the middle of the bathroom, talking to Max.

How did you get out there to the far boat? Did you step from plank to plank? Did your knees shake? Did the river hold its breath in case you slipped and fell, into its belly?

"Sssh". Max washes over her. His voice is water pouring out of every tap and it is such a comfort.

"Alice. Are you all right?" Maddy is at the door, but Alice won't be interrupted. Her eyes are closed as she leans into the steam of Max's warm embrace. She is enraptured, swooning. She is giving in to longing and she's more at ease with herself than she has been for months. And quite proud; she has conjured Max so easily.

I thought if I opened my mouth I would choke up shoals of dull grey fish who've swum beneath your boat for weeks until the slatted sky of their world drained all the colour from their scales and muddied up their eyes.

"Alice?"

But I opened wide and a river poured out, shimmery and new, and over my tongue it washed a little punt with you, the boatman, on it.

"Answer me, will you." Maddy knows a crisis when she hears one.

"I'm all right, thanks. Getting ready to go to bed." She opens the bathroom door to Maddy.

"What are you doing?" A rush of steam and water.

"Running a bath".

"Well – if you're sure – we're thinking of going now."

"Sure. I'm sure."

She is so sure she can hardly manage the watery smile. "Do you think they'll mind if I don't come down? I just want a quiet bath and fall into bed." And before Maddy can reply, Alice calls downstairs, "Goodnight everybody."

*

She has been meaning to dig a garden pond forever. She even has one of those hard plastic liners in the shed, nature shaped and a hideous green. Mr Hargreaves had been quite excited when she'd

51

mentioned it to him, months ago. He had said that a nature pond was A Good Thing and he had talked for over half an hour about the crested newt and the recent scarcity of the damsel fly. Alice is a sucker for approval, and Mr Hargreaves stirred in her a little surge of giddiness that day. She had fetched the pond to show him. But as soon as it appeared his face had fallen in and he'd sucked through his dentures as he talked her through the hazardous world of back-filling and the properties of thermoplastics. Alice had been thoroughly disheartened and ashamed, almost. She'd said "Oh dear, oh dear", in an oddly genteel, 1940's kind of voice, as Mr Hargreaves wandered off to do more pruning. The pre-formed pond has languished in her damp shed ever since.

She waits in the bathroom now, until she's sure her friends have gone. Then she puts the bathplug in and leaves the water running; she does the same with the sink and flushes the toilet for good measure as she hurries out, engulfed by Max, a cloud of steam in her wake. She's past the half-stacked dirty dishes, and into the coat cupboard: wellingtons, kagoul, thermal hat, back door key. Max. She eases the hat on gingerly because her head still aches and because she's absolutely certain now, and realises with a small shudder at the back of her waist, there is a ridge of something hard running along her skull, from front to back, as it were. She thinks for a second of the green Mohican that Malcolm Tillotson sported in 1985, but this is no haircut, Alice knows; it is the boat taking shape.

She begins to dig in the potato patch. The soil gives easily at first and the moon is high. She works for over an hour before she notices her hands are sore and she's thirsty. But she must press on. She's forgotten the pre-formed pond; (did she ever remember it?) this will be something bigger, better, something to transport her, to transport her and Max. They will be cast adrift in the wide wet world. She will not carry a boat on her tired head. No. She will make her own punt and they will lie in it together.

*

If he could wake up just enough to check the clock, Mr Hargreaves might know that he always needs to pee between the hours of 3 and 4am, regardless, it would seem, of whether or not he's had a bedtime cup of tea or Ovaltine or just a bowl of Shreddies with a splash of milk. Tonight he dreams of water rippling through his bedroom walls; a restful dream at first but then it's urgent and he's on his feet and stumbling to the toilet in the dark, almost a sleep walk.

In the morning, when he hears the terrible crack of next door's floor collapsing, and he opens, aghast, his very damp front door, he'll remember what he dreamt this night.

It's a dream that begins in his bathroom with a glimpse of the outside world as it hovers quietly under the still, bright moon. Where steps should lead from Alice's terrace to her lawn, there's a waterfall, torrential and magnificent, and where her garden used to be, a dark lake stares. There's a simple boat, little more than a wide plank, really (very like, in fact, a piece of Mr Hargreaves' own fence) with Alice and her lover on it. Lying on their backs together, they are holding hands and each trails an arm in the water.

All night, Mr Hargreaves hears the lap and drag of oars that scud the surface, and there's something else in the air. Brand new

53

waterways are opening up across the gardens, each one like a careful tear through silk; a map of waterways as far as the eye can see, beyond Bill Strick's allotments, even. Mr Hargreaves' thick hands clench a little as a memory washes up from somewhere far away. Forty years ago, the unexpected, secret touch of his dear beloved Mary. He watches, mesmerised, a ladder running through her tights, a quiet unravelling, unstoppable, over her ample thigh. There's a small hill on the horizon. As the sky lightens, Mr Hargreaves strains to see a little further through his bathroom window. And yes, it's possible to just make out a small boat, disappearing. Max and Alice, he knows, though he can no longer see them, drifting out beyond the hill, across the world, on water that is slightly creased and blurred and grey.

The Peacock's Dance
Tariq Mehmood

The peacock had not danced today. Allah Ditta knew it would
dance no more. But still he opened the window in time to see the
dance of the peacock. Perhaps there never was any peacock, or
any dance. He could not be sure, but there must have been
something of beauty, for how else did he have a peacock's feather.
And why did this feather pull him to itself? And why did it send
burning shock waves through his body when he rubbed it across
his face?

The peacock could dance no more. On that late summer
day he knew he had seen its last dance, and on that occasion it had
not stopped its dance even after looking down at its own feet. Nor
had he seen it shed its legendary tears. It was then that Allah Ditta
had wondered, perhaps youth had been a delusion, and friendship
its unfaithful companion - all trapped in a flimsy ribcage of time.

The peacock had danced its last. He had seen the three
boys coming out of the thick canopy of ivy that had been trained
over the rotting wooden fence behind which was held the outer
limit of Bracken Bank estate. They were young, perhaps only just
out of their teens. They too had been mesmerised by the dazzling
brilliance of the cascading psychedelic frenzy of the peacock's
ritual. Allah Ditta had seen them peering through the fence;
gaping at the dance of the peacock.

The peacock had opened its crown for the last time, its
circular shadow falling backwards over the freshly mowed lawn. It
must surely have been ignorant of the impending doom. Why else

would it have embraced the shade of a solitary cloud sliding above in an expanse of heavenly blue? Allah Ditta was to wonder this for the rest of his life. Whilst the shade of the cloud, slithered off the back of the dancing peacock, the three boys quickly ran across the streaks of the lawn and hid themselves under the protective arms of a weeping willow.

A strange stillness hung in the humid air of his damp room. It was broken by the frustrated cries of a fly, trapped behind the yellowing net curtains that were swaying gently, like a ripple in an old lake, as though a hidden hand was moving up and down. If it had not been for the fly, Allah Ditta may not have heard the sighs of the memories carried to him by a hot summer's wind.

"Why are you whispering pain in my ear?" Allah Ditta asked the wind as he looked at himself in the mirror. He did not fully recognise the balding white bearded old wreck of a man who grinned a mischievous youthful smile back at him. A small round face, with thin lips and a patchy silver beard looked out for someone who had withered away and ceased to be. He saw the quivering lips move and he said in protest, "Memories! Men in mirrors have no need of you."

Staring in the mirror he remembered those mischievously youthful eyes looking out of the window. For a moment he thought he saw the peacock dancing, but then shook his head in disbelief. A wave rippled through a curtain somewhere and he heard the fly buzzing louder and then it crashed against the glass and went silent for a moment. Just as he was about to turn away from the mirror, the fly noisily resumed its hunt for freedom. The wind whispered a ghostly lament into Allah Ditta's ears and he smiled with the thought that half a century or so ago, before coming to England, he had thought that this country was so clean that there were no flies here.

Drawing the net curtains back Allah Ditta only

confirmed that which he already knew. There would be no dance today. Sticking his head out of the window, Allah Ditta inhaled the scent of jasmine flowers. He felt the scent burning a hole in his body as it went deeper and deeper into his soul. He began to drift back to another time.

It had been the end of a day in which the relentless heat of the summer had been broken by the first droplets of the monsoons. It had rained after many months and the earth was thirsty. Even the birds of the rugged red brown hills surrounding his village had stopped singing, perhaps in anticipation of the rains proper. Or maybe Allah Ditta had thought they, like him, had been intoxicated by the fresh fumes of the dry earth being hit by the first raindrops.

He used to meet his Beloved in a small crevice of the snaking hills in whose palm sat his village. Children of the village lived in awe of the crevice. It was said by the wise departed, that each year, just before the beginning of the monsoons, the Moar, a mysterious peacock, used to come and spread its feathers, waiting for its lover. But she could only come to him, but for a moment, once every hundred years. And his love was so strong that he waited and waited. Finally the day of the reunion arrived. But evil men, from distant lands, talking in strange tongues came and captured the Moarni and took her away. She was never seen again. The loss of his lover made the Moar's heart explode inside his chest and his feathers flew out of his body and scattered into the hills. Lovers have searched for these ever since.

Unlike other children, Allah Ditta and Zakia had no fear of the crevice and, against the wishes of their parents, had always played in it. Once when he had been around sixteen, Zakia had had to leave the village for a few weeks. Allah Ditta had gone to the crevice in the middle of the night and played his flute till just before dawn. The children of the village started to believe that the Moar had returned and was singing for his Moarni.

Just after the last Azaan, when the faithful went to pray at the village mosque, Zakia had worn a peacock feather in the knot of her jasmine oiled black hair. Drops of sweat shone like pearls on her soft dark skin. He declared his life's dream to her.

"You cannot get to England," Zakia said light heartedly. Her flaming eyes shining under a blazing full moon. With a quick dexterous movement she caught a glowworm. Her fist glowed in its desire. Letting it go she said, "See, tandarnas never let go of their light."

"There is nothing a man cannot do if he should set his mind it," Allah Ditta mused stroking the feather.

"An aajri, who plays his flute to please shadows," Zakia said pulling the bamboo instrument out of the top pocket of his kurta, "how can someone like him, without two annas, raise rupees?" She rubbed the flute through his dark curly hair. Raising it skywards she drew an ark in the air. The flute cried.

"I need no ticket." Allah Ditta sulked falsely pulling Zakia's thin body into a tight embrace. Closing his eyes he descended into a joyous silence, inhailing deeply the jasmine in Zakia's freshly washed hair.

"Will an angel take you to England?" Zakia asked, pushing him away only to adjust herself closer to his moist body.

"Silly!" Allah Ditta sniggered. Something slimy rubbed against his foot. "Snake!" Allah Ditta shouted in terror, "Cobra!"

"Shh, now," Zakia said calmly brushing dust off her long thin arms. "Snakes don't sting lovers." Shaking grit out of her chapples she added, "Unless they forsake love."

"What else can I do?" Allah Ditta asked sullenly

"You will do here what you will do there."

"How will I ever make a home?"

"God will help."

"How will I marry you?"

"We are already married. God is my witness."

"I have to do what I have to do," Allah Ditta said in a soft voice whose journey to Zakia's ears a whistling wind had interrupted.

Zakia returned a forlorn smile.

They remained in a deep, love-filled, silent embrace. Glow-worms flickered about them. The sound of the village heaving into life rose up in an unintelligible cacophonony above the lovers, like a dark rumbling monsoon cloud, which only threatens to shed itself and then passes.

Zakia had found the peacock's feather, by the side of the GT road, stuck in the thorns of a wild bush, but she had lied to Allah Ditta, telling him she had found it in the crevice. Of course, he knew this not to be the truth, but this sweet lie, tasted so good, that he would not exchange it for anything in the world.

A few days after this meeting Zakia had given Allah Ditta a gold bracelet that had been passed down through the generations to her. He had given this as a deposit to the agent, with the promise of sending money back to him, so that Zakia could take it back.

Their last clandestine meeting of love had been brief and solemn. It was the night before he was leaving for England. The whole village had come to say their farewells. Just after the last Azaan, he had left for the crevice and there waiting for him had been Zakia, with wet eyes, shining in the moonlight.

"No words my love," Zakia had said, "I have given you all I have and I have cried for both of us." Plucking the peacock feather out of her hair she had placed it gently in his hand. Before he had had a chance to say anything she had turned around and slipped out of the crevice disappearing into a swarm of glow-worms.

A few drops of rain fell down from the cloudless English sky and pattered on Allah Ditta's head, chasing away with its coming the swarms of memories meandering in his mind. Taking a deep laboured breath he became conscious of the imprisoning embrace of the jasmine. He held his breath for a while and then slowly let out a tired sigh as he tried to free himself from the scented clasp. It was futile. A thick sticky aroma started gnawing the back of his throat. He was leaning out of the window, with his clenched fist shaking by the ledge.

The sun was now gleaming off the tops of tall erect poplars that stood uniformly along the western wing of the gardens. A halo of light hung over the tips of the trees and the sun peeped through the branches. Straining his eyes he tried to find the glow-worms from that crevice of his youth, now floating in the poplars. But it was only the winking sun, twinkling in between the leaves, swaying to the moans of an easterly wind. Allah Ditta tried to dive back into the sweet taste of the shadows now floating in his head. Alas, those melodious memories of the crevice of his love, drowned into a blank void in which he now slipped. The taste of the jasmine continued to linger on, with the scent whisked away by the winds.

With the fading scent of the jasmine, Allah Ditta felt the world around him being drained of sound. Closing his large quivering eyes, he felt the wind tickling his thick silver brows. Raising his head skywards he inhaled deeply, taking in a faint lost whiff of jasmine, that had somehow lingered on in-between the crossing winds. After holding his breath for a few moments he opened his eyes, half expecting to see his old friend, dancing, in the same spot that had now been burnt in his memory. The wind went silent. The trees moved ever so quietly. No birds sang. The peacock was not dancing. The silence was so intense that it rang like a tuning fork inside his head. He felt a strange burning sorrow rumbling in his gut. It was sorrow tied down by loss. Of what, he could no longer articulate. Nor did he fully understand the reason why he rushed to block out all memories of that which he wanted to remember. Something in his clenched hand was burning into his skin. Allah Ditta tried to open his fist. A tremor ran through his leathery hand. A voice inside his head warned,

"Festering wounds never heal."

A sudden gust of wind violently shook the leaves of the poplars. The sun flickered. A bird screamed somewhere in the branches. He knew the scream well. But this was the only time he had heard it flushed with a joyous anguish - of a soul being released from bondage. Allah Ditta looked into the blinking branches with sparkling leaves, searching for a glimpse of his old friend. But he knew he would not find him. As the scream faded, Allah Ditta managed to open his hand, and there, in his palm, stuck in heavy sweat, almost covering the deep gorges in the valley of his hand was a withering peacock feather.

"And why have you not spread your crown and danced for me today?" Allah Ditta whispered into the wind. The edges of the feather began to separate and flicker gently. Allah Ditta answered what he thought was a question brought in by the wind, "I knew you did not want to be warned. Is that not so Beloved?" He waited for an answer and recalled the moment when he had seen the last dance of the peacock.

The three boys had sat under the weeping willow and had not moved as the peacock started to dance. The cloud above the peacock's shadow thinned out and began to disperse. The boys made their move. They rushed from their hiding place and spread out in different directions, encircling the dancing peacock. Then, ever so slowly, they advanced.

The soft wind played a warm enchanting wail, to which the peacock turned in Dervishish harmony. The boys had seen Allah Ditta looking out at them. But they knew there was nothing an old wreck could do. As the boys got closer to the peacock, Allah Ditta had felt his throat tightening. Raising his unsteady hand he had been about to shout a warning to the peacock. Seeing this, the boys stopped in their tracks. The peacock looked across at Allah Ditta and he felt a surge of joy racing through his body. But words left him. The boys waited for a few moments, and then raced towards the peacock. One of them threw a large white net curtain over the bird. The other two pounced on it. The peacock had given in without protest. After fastening the peacock's legs with a thick nylon rope, the boys began to pluck the feathers out of its body. It was only then that the peacock had cried and Allah Ditta understood that cry. Why should the peacock have to live bereft of the beauty of its crown? Once they finished tearing the feathers out of the peacocks, the boys tied their booty into a large bundle inside the net curtains and left laughing. They tossed the bleeding body into a rubbish bin.

By the time Allah Ditta reached the place of the peacock's dethroning, the boys had long since gone. Their laughter lingered on in the air, fading with the peacock's screams.

"I won't desert you," Allah Ditta said raising his arm towards the rubbish bin. Lifting the lid off the bin Allah Ditta looked straight into the eyes of the peacock. The peacock closed its eyes dejectedly and turned its head away. "Come my friend," Allah Ditta said in a soft voice tempered with the harshness of age. "I will nurse you."

Allah Ditta lowered himself into the bin and reached out for the peacock. The peacock turned its head round and opened its eyes as Allah Ditta's hand touched its body. He felt its terror race through his body. He felt the world around him beginning to spin as he heard a muzzled voice from somewhere deep in the shadowy mists of his mind. Slowly, ever so slowly, a voice, not human, but humanely soothing, like the note of a flute, trapped in the crevice of some hills, continued to echo upwards. Getting closer and closer with the passing of each second. It was as though the flute was playing and the notes were being carried by the wind.

"Why did this have to happen to me here?" The voice asked. It became clearer with the uttering of each word, until it sang its own melody so clearly that Allah Ditta felt he was a part of the voice itself. He understood that the peacock had at last decided to talk to him. The peacock in his hand did not move its beak. Lovers do not need words.

"There is no answer to this question," Allah Ditta answered.

"Why did they take her from me?" The peacock asked. "We had waited for a hundred years for our momentary re-union."

"You had no need to come to this cold, cold place," Allah Ditta said.

"It was destined so. But why did you watch my dance every year?"

"In your open wings, I saw my Beloved's accusing eyes and behind shadows of your outstretched crown, I saw her spirit moving."

"I was just praying for one last glimpse of my soul's enslaver."

"And what became of your prayers?"

"My dance was my prayer and I am before you still praying. But why did you watch my dance alone?"

"I am alone."

"What of your children?"

"My children!" Allah Ditta felt a sudden prickly shock run through his body as his mind flashed back toward a time

65

before, somewhere else. When the grey bearded man was yet a youth. "My children," Allah Ditta repeated to himself as faces without names, in shapeless bodies flashed through his mind. Each one filling him with memories that turned sour before he had had time to savour their sweetness.

"Yes, your children. Where..."

"Only one child." Another voice interrupted the peacock.

Allah Ditta trembled in terror, but then a reunited lover's warmth rushed through his being as he recognised Zakia. She was saying,

"Only one child I had and that was yours. But those wolves, who parade as yesterday's protectors and tomorrow's guardians, fed it to stray dogs, and this on that day when Allah let him breathe his first breath. And still you did not come back."

Allah Ditta tried to run away into another voice, but wherever he turned he was engulfed by Zakia's word. "I was trapped in debt, beloved. All I wanted to do was to repay that, build a house and then come back to you."

"But your house was built and still you did not come back," Zakia said.

"It could not be finished, for my mill closed down and I could find no other work."

"But you did find other work and I still waited and still you did not come back."

"Yes, but Cousin Hamza was getting married, and cousin Sarah was in hospital and uncle Majid's only son accidentally killed a man in Saudi, and I had to pay for all these and many more."

"You did all that and you still did not come back."

"I was coming when they opened the gates of Mangla Dam without any warnings and my house was washed away in those waters that had been forcibly imprisoned for so long.'

"Those waters subsided."

"I became unworthy of you."

"Though I would always have felt betrayal's pangs, my love would have forgiven you."

"Then children came."

"I would have accepted them too."

"You too left this world."

"Fat has covered your eyes. We could have lived in a house of straw and it would have been bonded in our love, which would withstand any hurricane. We could've had that which foreign lands can never give. We could have changed our own world, and if we had failed trying to do this, then we would have failed together and not suffered separation's embrace. We could've planted in our children's dreams that they could have had whilst awake. They too could have gone to our crevice of legends. But you became bewitched by a world you didn't even know. A world of bewitching things. A sweet prison... of tortured dreams."

"We will meet soon," Allah Ditta said.

Allah Ditta waited for a reply but there was only a resentful void. The peacock broke the silence,

"Youth only has beauty if it can change its own time and life only has meaning trying to save Beloved. Now my friend, farewell."

Coming back to consciousness Allah Ditta had stared deeply into the peacock's eyes for one last time and then with a quick movement of tired hands he had wrenched its life.

The moist feather in Allah Ditta's hand was all but free from the chains of his sweat. He could see an outline of the peacock dancing. It was there, floating in the air above the head of the male nurse who was pushing an old wheelchair bound man.

"Your son phoned earlier Mr Ditta and said he is very busy and won't be able to visit you today." The nurse shouted across to Allah Ditta as he passed by his window.

Allah Ditta heard a fly buzzing in the curtains and then he saw it escaping skywards. Just then a sudden gust of wind washed the peacock's feather out of Allah Ditta's trembling hand. He watched the feather, twisting and turning, spiralling upwards, and upwards. Placing his emptied hand into his pocket he pulled out a gold bracelet and kissed it gently. A few tears rolled out of his bloodshot eyes.

Nocturne
Michael Bracewell

"Lighten our darkness, we beseech thee, O Lord; and by thy great
mercy defend us from all perils and dangers of this night..."
The Third Collect; Order for Evening Prayer

I know what I would like to describe: a winter's evening on the
edge of the city, back in the early 1990s.

The three wide-screen TVs, transmitting the match as a
booming succession of putty-hued scenes, hung like divided altar
panels above the length of the sports club bar. Slumped in over-
stuffed armchairs, or sitting on high-polished stools, a dozen or so
drinkers were following the game with varied expressions of
tension, irritation or boredom. The covers on the chairs were
printed with an intricate pattern of pallid pink stripes and silver
leaves, worn smooth and faded through constant use. On the
stools, the drinkers sat with their arms folded like weights pulling
down from drooped shoulders.

Here and there, on low tables with mosaic surfaces of
green and white tiles, the remains of snack lunches and dregs of
drinks looked as though they'd been there for a while. Crumpled
paper napkins were stuffed in the shallow baskets which had held
garlic bread or chips; empty glasses, ringed with descending tide
marks of dried beer foam, or housing the shrunken crescents of
sliced lemons, showed greasy thumb prints. A young waiter, little
more than a boy, who had a thin grey face and narrow eyes, and

71

his short black hair greased up into vertical spikes, was holding his breath as he carried a tray laden with dirty coffee cups towards the swing door which led to the kitchen. The drinkers, watching a fumbled pass, let out a sudden gasp which turned into a moan of disappointment; their exhalation fell like the roar of surf sucked back through loose shingle. The young waiter faltered, checked his balance, and then resumed his nervous journey.

The bar was a long, low-ceilinged room, with wide-paned windows which ran at waist-height down one wall. The room, unlit, would have seemed cold and functional were it not for the jumping glare of the television sets as it played across the upturned faces and threw blocks of shadow across the peach-coloured wallpaper. A torn ribbon of blue tissue paper, left over from the decorations for a Christmas party, shivered on a high current of air. The windows, all shut, looked out on to a low hedge of rhododendron bushes: their dark, waxy leaves reflected thin spines of light. The polished teak structure of the bar itself had an upper shelf containing a selection of shabby, second hand books, ranged to either side of an antique clock. The names of the clock's manufacturer, 'Hawkins of Preston' was printed across its face in small black letters.

The room was warm, and the atmosphere heavy with the smell of fried food, cigarette smoke and beer. At the far end, through a pair of glass doors, you could just see the club's deserted hallway where a vending machine glowed in the grey light of mid afternoon.

Two women, one blonde, the other brunette, were half lying in the pair of armchairs which stood furthest from the bar. The brunette, who had been rubbing her forehead with the middle finger of her right hand as she gazed towards one of the television screens, drew heavily on a long cigarette before exhaling two flared streams of smoke through her nose. Her legs were stretched out in front of her, and her feet were resting on the end of the coffee table. She was wearing a voluminous tracksuit, and a thick-soled pair of white sports shoes. She felt and looked overweight. Her hair was brown, falling to her shoulders in heavy ringlets. A half finished glass of grapefruit juice was standing on the table beside her heavy bunch of keys, which were fastened to a swatch of navy blue leather with a gold ring stitched to its centre. Pale, with brown eyes, her features seemed to have fallen to a set pattern of lethargic cynicism, as though life could no longer surprise her. Her name was Sofia Adele Cartwright, and her friend called her Sofe.

Now in her late thirties, people might think that Sofia's youth had curdled inside her, souring the expression of maturity. Her girlish engagement ring - a tiny solitaire diamond on a fragile band of silver - was trapped beneath the heavier stones of her wedding ring, which was wedged against the slack skin of her knuckle. She settled deeper into her chair, and stared back up towards the nearest screen without blinking, stroking her raised chin with her thumb.

Beside her, curled up with her knees pressed together and cupping the side of her face on her hand, the brunette's companion was narrow-shouldered and small boned. Her name was Josephine Smith, but this had been reduced to simply Jo for as long as anyone could remember. She was dressed in black leggings and a long, shapeless pullover which held the powdery scent of her sweet perfume. Her fragile face, with its slightly hooked nose and pointed chin was drawn and tanned. Where Sofia looked cynical, Jo looked worn out. There were blue shadows of fatigue beneath her bright, sparrow-like eyes. Her shoulders were hunched, as though she was permenantly cold, and her bearing seemed to indicate obedience as much as her friend's did defiance. Her mouth was set in a sad smile, which appeared to be held in place by a constant effort of will. When she withdrew into her own thoughts, the smile disappeared as though it was worthless; called back to attention, the smile returned, but it was confounded by an expression behind the brightness of her eyes as if she was smiling from far away towards people who could never reach her.

The commentator's chattering about constantly up-dated facts was ceaseless. His voice was a sturdy monotone; the three wide screens, split down their middles, now, like an experimental movie, were displaying an accelerating sequence of photographs of footballers. The names of the players, their ages, teams and positions, were listed in urgent italicised capitals down one side, wavering to a blur at their edges on a bright green background. Putting her head to one side, Jo began to rub the nape of her neck with her fingertips - they felt cold - in a gentle circular motion. She could feel the light weight of her corn blonde hair as it hung towards her shoulder. Wearily, but with the casual interest of a person whose attention has just been caught, she studied the changing gallery of red, dependable faces. She could see why Sofia, a few minutes earlier, had said that they all looked like photos of the same bloke.

Watching the procession of grinning young men, Jo's caramel-coloured eyes showed no emotion. But her mind was turning over, with the same barely conscious sense of resignation that she experienced while folding blankets, alone in the master bedroom of her over-heated house, the thought that these young men were all pampered - preening and pampered... It made her think of the time before she was married, all those years ago, when she had studied the low-browed anonymity of a thousand young men who might be gathered in the scarlet half light of deafening clubs and bars. So long ago.

With scented ringlets, squaddies' crops or centre partings, boyish cheek or Latin bravado, those young men had presented a collective of masculinity - their very ordinariness was what made them so attractive, and their lack of distinction, taken together,

had been somehow exciting - the thrilled pulse of her universe. At
nineteen, she had been engaged to a footballer. She had been a
trainee beautician - she winced to think of it now - and he, well
he *had* been heading for the top of the tree. She knew about
footballers. At night, watching them besuited and polite on the
mid-week round-up, she could almost smell their cologne and the
hot bed linen of their junior suites, taut and crisp in the gloaming
of a wide-shaded lamp. They were born to sport, and then dipped
in the developing fluid of department store glamour. Here were
the grins of cheerful salesmen in adverts for DIY superstores; an
earring, a chipped tooth, a day or so's nurtured stubble, might hint
at the shallows of fame - but their lives, she knew, were as
corporate as carpet tiles and air conditioning. And now she was
married to someone in enviromental health.

Jo would be thirty five in August; that would make
seventeen years since she had sat, obedient and bewildered, on the
edge of a queen-sized bed in some slab of a hotel, and listened to
Chris Ryanagh tell her why she was there from the steam-filled
cell of the en-suite bathroom. It had still been early in the evening.
She hadn't been able to see him. When he had emerged, still
talking, he was stripped to the waist and patting the moistened
skin of his freshly shaved cheeks with the end of the towel draped
over his shoulders. The warm smell of cloves had pursued him,
rich in the clearing steam. His confidence had appalled her. It
seemed inevitable that he should win.
"I do wish he wouldn't do that."

Jo's smile switched on as she turned towards Sofia. The
voice had reached her from a funnel of darkness.

"Do what?" Her face became a mask of attentiveness.

"That thing - " Sofia laughed, "That thing with his nuts.."

Still smiling, Jo followed her friend's line of vision to
where a portly young man was sitting at the bar; he was wearing a
pale blue shirt with short sleeves, and throwing back his large,

ginger-haired head as he swallowed the last fragments of peanuts from a bowl.

"He's just been flicking them in, one after another, non-stop. And I don't want to watch him gulping them down. God.." Sofia's voice trailed away to a groan of disgust. It was her usual tone. The sky could darken, raining fire on the red roofs of Whitefields, an apocalypse could burst its onion of scarlet flame in the windows of Hexagon House - the petrochemical manufacturers, just beyond Sofia's back garden - flashing horizontal white light towards the M62, and still, Jo thought, Sofia would sigh at the complacent habits of a gormless male God and say that she just didn't know. To Sofia, it seemed, all men who weren't stupid were liars, and the rest were less capable than infants at running the business of life. Men were a broken promise, to be treated as frauds. So why, Jo wondered, did Sofia find them so necessary? For reassurance against the tide of time and age? Boredom? It was anyone's guess, really.

The match was over, the TVs mute. The members of the sports club who had come together two hours earlier, not meaning to linger but settling into temporary domesticity like travellers on a long-haul flight, were rising and stretching to a new formality. Jo, also rousing herself, looked around at the faces she knew. There was Phil Clark, and Helen's husband, Ken, and Trevor. The man with the nuts was tucking his shirt into the back of his beige trousers. Everyone dressed like rappers nowadays. The metallic strap of his diver's watch was digging into the bulge of grey flesh above his wrist. She sat up straight and patted her thighs in a gesture of decisiveness. Sofia, leaning over the arm of her chair, was reaching for the zip of her sports bag.

"I only meant to stop a minute, " she said, slightly breathless from her strained position, "but once I sat down I felt shattered." Her face creased into a sudden yawn, her mouth a stretched oval. "I did 'Commit To Get Fit' and I've only been

76

twice. Spend a bloody fortune on a track suit and I only wear it round the house - hey, Ken!"

A tall man, sandy haired with dark, heavy eyebrows and a pleased expression stopped by the edge of the bar. He flexed his leg, as Sofia began to tease him - wait until she told Helen, what about the kids and that back bedroom? I don't know... He seemed to be enjoying the attention. An awkward trio, the three of them left the bar.

The smell of cigarettes gaveway to the exhilarating scent of cold air and damp, let in through the club-house doors to the lobby. Jo wanted to be on her own, and told the others to go on ahead while she made a phone call. But there was no one for Jo to call, even as she mimed the performance of searching for change in her soft black purse. Through the wall of the function room, the bump of bass from that night's dinner and dance sounded for a few seconds as the DJ tested his decks.

It was the third Saturday in March. Outside, marking the rim of the carpark, which had been rebuilt the previous year around illuminated islands of solitary caged saplings, the swollen spears of a new season's daffodils were thrusting from tarred tubs. The light had lingered, dyeing the dusk pale blue. It was intensely cold. Above the gardens of the neighbouring houses, just loose from the grip of winter but still long distant from the care of the owners, a cliff of black cloud lay low in the sky. Jo stopped to look at the setting sun: a bright yolk, poached in ash, it seemed to descend with a rumble of anger behind the suburban horizon, somewhere towards the moors.

Sitting in the warm twilight of her car, inhaling the smell of new leather, she watched the scattering of luminous green lights which had turned the dashboard into a firmament; the engine was virtually soundless - a flutter of hidden strength as she touched the hard angle of the acclerator with her toe. As the heavy vehicle swung with inappropriate lightness towards the darkening estuary of tree lined streets, leading to the floodlit mouth of the motorway, Jo caught a glimpse of herself in the past. The memory was triggered by a particular constellation of orange streetlight, dark curb and the awareness of brighter streets ahead - as though a busy city precinct lay where in fact the illuminated emptiness of the northbound motorway began. It was, Jo felt, like acute deja vu for a dream which she could barely remember, but with each heavy second the atmosphere of the dream became stronger, eclipsing her short-term memory...

The bench was cold and wet through her thin skirt; she was slightly drunk, enjoying herself. Her seventeenth birthday, was it? Jo connected the memory to a scent of rosemary, richly green, which had risen from the three shiny white tablets of soap - a present from her grandmother. The soaps fitted neatly into their cardboard box, with a lid of sharp-edged cellophane. The gift had matched the girlish order of her old bedroom, and her ruling deity of perfumed cleanliness. In spring, at her parents' house, the light outside - as though it was freshly washed itself - had shown up the dirt of a long winter on the window panes. It made her nervous and ill-tempered - sad to face the weight of fate. The horn of her father's car had scattered pigeons in a splash of pale sunshine, driving Jo to work on her first morning. There was the unbearable sadness of the magpie which had lost its mate, returning to the same bough of the tree beyond her window, at the same time, every day, its complete fidelity crushed by cruelty. Some time later her fiance would give up football because he said his surname was one syllable too long to become famous.

She had been leaning forward, clasping her sides with her arms tightly folded across her chest, and turning to shout something towards someone. Behind her, floodlit, the imposing facade of the town hall, indented with pitch black quadrants of shadow. Beside her feet an opened bottle of sweet white wine. The tepid rain, just starting, made her shiver. The northern July had turned wet after three weeks of stifling humidity. A hot brown arm, rough with hair, had rested on her shoulder, but it had less significance than the rain. She had seen the young man's eyes, filled with hope. A car had pulled away, its impudent horn sounding a deafening arpeggio, heralding its high revs to the next set of lights. Soon they were marching five abreast towards the crowded doorway of a club, where purple light fell in a fanned triangle across a short stretch of wet pavement, turning brown hair black and flushed faces white, caught up in an ecstatic pushing and shoving to the darkened interior.

Shouting and coloured light. As the party made its way, in the crush of the noisy crowd, towards a staircase which descended between black-painted walls, Jo had caught a glimpse of herself, of them all, upside down in the mirrors on the ceiling. She couldn't work out the reflection, feeling herself pushed forward by hot, impatient hands. They had bought her a cocktail from the thatched bar - a pint glass filled with a rum-smelling liquid, the colour of rose wine. This was back in the days of disco. She held it, undrinkable, to the slide of strings and the beat four on the floor. A boy had shouted in her ear: "If there was an operation to become black, yeah? I'd have it. I would."

Her friends would have liked her to be drunk, at first; then it seemed that they needed her to be drunk, to pass out, perhaps. She was required to become an anecdote. This order was supreme in every atom of the dark club, not spoken; should she not fall into line, she would commit a heresy which would be seen to rip a fissure across not only the party, but all the parties, and all the preparations for all the parties that ever had been or ever would be. Without her acquiescence, the chain of the universe would snap; and Sofia would never sit in the sports club bar and flirt pointlessly with Ken while a young spring night turned bitterly cold.

How to make sense of this long perspective into darkness? The horizontal straightahead, as an illusion, like the slow descent of the motorway from Liverpool could suddenly seem like a vertical plunge down sheer walls of grey concrete. Beneath high white lights, the grass embankment looked grey. Black clouds were pressing down on the final stratum of cream-coloured sunset. Jo, glancing left, could glimpse the freezing desolation of a wilderness. The motorway was its own country, a new rendition of a prehistoric theme - beyond the times of settlements or service stations, silent mining villages or the vast illuminated glass palace of the mothership retail park... Jo imagined she was driving.

The Importance of the North West
Anthony Wilson

It was the noise. Low, incessant, gently whirring. It was the noise that was his only true suffering. The only price to pay for turning the world on its head. It seemed to him that he could escape everything except the absence of silence. And so silence became his obsession.

His persecutors were a little bit Lou Reed, a little bit John Adams.

The metal machine music was the air-conditioning, the air-feeding. Vague intimations of metal against metal. But if you must live underground there was no choice. 'I breathe therefore I am' is a truth even philosophers accede to. And the sand of the Hadhramaut plain, a few feet above his fluorescent bedecked ceiling was probably at 120 degrees right now. Hot outside. Oh yes, very hot outside.

And the counterpoint to the whirring was a slow steady pulse, the pulsations that replace beat in contemporary classical. No not the Texas state orchestra, this interference came from the steely businesslike dialysis machine perched on the medical table in the corner of his great square room. No-one used the word bunker. A forbidden reference.

His room was a perfect square, fifty feet by fifty feet, dominated by a great oak table which filled the centre of the space. On the table, words, words, words. Books in little piles scattered on one side; newspapers, journals, web print outs covering the other side. And the heap of press cuttings from what was left of his PR operation in Jeddah. There were even colour photo shoots. He was the stuff of the regions *OK* and *Hello*. Stardom hardly sat easy with his modest, quietly earnest demeanour. But stardom and the family construction business were his game. His other game.

All else was light and airy. The openness enhanced by great oblong windows on every side of his temporary home. Windows on the world. Great flat screens of liquid crystals. Each screen/window was fed by two cameras pointing to the four quarters of the earth. Not on a North-South axis. Of course not. The perfect cube was set on a vaguely North-West skew. His front windows setting a line straight to his personal Damascus. That pilgrimage that forever buried his fears and the top-line Mercs and Johnny Walker Black Label that had for a while muffled those fears.

The cameras feeding his limited vision were tiny little minicams, no more than perspex eyes at the end of wound cable, hidden in small desert rocks placed directly above their receptor screens. He was assured they were invisible to the prying eyes which pried from a hundred miles away.

In the middle of the South-East wall, a steel door gave out into a vestibule and then a tunneled staircase down into the complex. As well as the women, there was living and working space for a small army. They got the remnants of Arthur's Knights into a small piece of rock in North-West England, sleeping, ready to wake when Albion needed them. So why not here? His small army was not the only remnant but he knew they would all soon be needed. The network would be switched on again when needed.

His reading was disturbed. "Coffee, sir".

He signalled the young man in. As the dark caffeine was placed near his left arm, he thought of his own sons and his wife. How long, fifteen months, sixteen. He prayed again, as he did so often, in habit and fear, he prayed they were safe up there in the North

West Frontier. The hill villa in the wooded mountains outside Peshawar was isolated and well protected. But still he prayed. Every day he prayed.

But he was here and they were there because they were all his children. All who suffered. What was that word in which his critics bathed? 'Cowardly'. Now there was obvious bollocks. No, it was 'fanatical'. Implied madness. Is a father mad to defend his children? Is a father fanatical? For my child I will kill. For my children I have killed.

He prayed again.

The sun was setting in his vision, across the great TVs that lined his existence. In the North West screens they made the great yellowing towers of Shibam glow and burn in orange flames, their white alabaster tops sucking up the last of the sun and pushing forward from the cliff faces that formed a crusted backdrop.

Ten miles away, they lined the horizon of his forward view.

For how many centuries had the powerful and the arrogant built their celebrations towards the heavens. San Gimignano and Bologna in the Italian way and for the Lords of Arabia five hundred years ago the same claims made in clay and sweat.

They called Shibam "the Manhattan of the Desert". Irony was not his thing but he got it nevertheless.

Another knock on the door. The creaking of steel sheets against their hinges. Always noises, never silence.

"Sir, the Al Jazeera crew are set up. Are you ready?"

All on Video
David Constantine

Straight after breakfast they watched the video. It seemed funny to leave the table just like that and funnier still, when it was only morning, to go through into the other room; but they did, as though for an adventure.

After breakfast, the flat day stretching ahead, was Leonard's bad time, or one of them; so Madge bustled, with an eye on him. Leave the curtains, said Betty. It will be more like the pictures. They switched the standard lamp on and the fire. Vic took his oblong out and went to the slot under the good-sized television. Never used it, said Leonard, a bit shame-faced. First time, eh? said Vic. Vic knew how. In it went, no problem. You never forget the first time, he said; but felt, as always, that he was wasted, with his fun, on Leonard. Still, he found the right little button on the remote control and they settled down, Vic between the ladies on the sofa, Leonard in an easy chair, and though it was early morning they sat back in a dim light with the coals on low to watch the video of Sally's wedding.

Abruptly, and in silence, there were legs in a suit, two ankle socks, and a long flame-coloured dress; then the upper halves, at an angle. We're in the garden, Vic said. Behind the registry office. Redhot pokers, a weeping willow, and the couple and the little girl were posing, but as if on the deck of a ship in a tilting gale. Don't worry, said Vic. It settles down. Then the sound came on, like an abattoir. The women shut their ears. Vic bent over the other little buttons. I've got my wrong glasses on, he said. Don't worry, it quietens down. I expect we did make a din, said Betty. Happiness, so that's what happiness sounds like, or hope, the hope for it, the determined hope for happiness this time, after last time, everybody hoping for the best, very loud. Leonard saw himself, joining in. He was shaking hands with the young man and lifting up the child who knew she was the princess of it all in a white frock with her pigtails and bouquet. The next shots were disconsolate, the party trailing away down the common pavement. But Vic said he liked that, didn't they? The party trailing away smaller and smaller until they reached the off-licence where they turned left and vanished. Harder than it looks, said Vic. You have to hold it steady. He had also got the traffic in, and strangers, creatures, swam up very close and swam away.

Then the thing went haywire, like a kaleidoscope with migraine. Sorry about this, said Vic. Me running after you and tripping up. In fact by the time he had seen to himself and taken a drink and sent out for a part, the hours of life had hurried on, the meal was ending, the speeches had begun, and there was Leonard trying to say, since it was only family and close friends, that anyone might make a mistake, in little things and in great things, and now by good fortune this was a new beginning. There he was, doing without his notes, trying to say it even better, and there was Madge beside him, willing him on, praying he wouldn't falter and lose his voice and turn her way with a look of dread and blankness, so that he felt ashamed, there in the almost dark behind closed curtains, that he should ever have been the cause of such a worry in another person's face. Sally replied. She had said all along she would answer back whatever the conventions were and so she did, standing between her child and her new husband. Men, she began. And so it went on: father, husband, father of little Gwen whom she hugged in a comradely fashion three or four times while she spoke. Here Vic had done very well. His magic eye dwelled on face after face and there wasn't one knew quite what to look like listening to Sally's speech. Two words - bitter springs - came up in Madge from the depths of long ago; then the rest, the whole line they belonged in: Mirth that hath no bitter springs; and the picture wobbled in her tears and not because Vic had not held steady. And Betty, who on the occasion - she was sure she had - had felt very sorry for her sister Madge and Leonard who after all had taken the girl back in and the baby too and were heartbroken now in the empty house, Betty watching it on video filled with bitterness and said again to herself: Where's the justice? And: Our Christine would have turned out nicer if she'd lived. On all the faces was a willingness to smile and laugh. All they all wanted was to be able to laugh and not feel bad. You never saw a gallery of faces showing so much willingness. Though in the end it was more like pleading: that the pretty young woman whose wedding day it was would say at least one thing they could feel all right about. Some nice shots, don't you think? said Vic. Ethel, for instance. Freddy with his medals.

How much more is there? Leonard asked. He had got up suddenly and was over by the curtains making a chink between them and looking out. There's the party yet, said Vic. The party, said Leonard. What's the weather doing, Len? Madge asked. His voice had gone funny. It seemed trapped in his chest, as though his jaws and his teeth were barred against it. She knew he was struggling when she heard that sort of voice. The weather? he said. The weather's not so good. Madge reached out from the settee to bring him back into his easy chair. We can fastforward if you're getting bored, said Vic. It starts with the grounds and everyone arriving. Well I'm enjoying it, said Betty.

Fastforwarding crazed the screen and through a mithering interference the figures of humans came together, embraced and went apart at manic speed. Is that the dancing? Betty asked. Not yet, said Vic. Leastways he didn't think so. Hard to tell at that speed. Slow down then. He slowed and at once out of a confusion by which the eyes and the ears and even more so the mind were greatly tormented there came order, a wonderfully fluid, generous, shifting and various order, a delight. The jazz had begun. In a rush Leonard had back the happiness it had occasioned in him then. He was blind with tears. That's it, he said in himself. That's us at our best. He meant the ability, the sovereign gift and free bestowing of it on all who cared to listen and receive. And the interplay, the courteous, easygoing give and take. The way the pianist, a youngish man with a face like the moon (a moon with specs on) and his bit of hair in a ponytail, the way he nodded in the singer, her black hair how copious and beautiful! and the trumpeter, a gent, how he let her through, and the aloof bass went steady and she then to and fro against the pianist in a loving contest set her voice, smiling as she raised the blues, and he smiled back, the smiles of people who can do it, they know they can, they have gifts to spare, they knew each other and surprised each other, an edge in her voice suddenly, suddenly a sadder flattening under his hands, and then the horn came in, asking for space and at once allowed it, came in tilting his trilby, and reached up sobbing and howling to a sadness beyond the love duet, and the bass approached, more agitated, more in haste now, more on his mind, the blues, distress, and pianist and girl backed off for the necessary while, until it was over, the sadness, got over with, over and done with, and what was wanted was full measure again, voice and the instruments, all in concert, all in the triumphant joyfulness of their ability, and finished, laughing. Us at our best, that give and take, no bossing, everyone unique, in an order of our devising and our accepting. And when you looked around, as Vic's roving eye made possible, the room seemed a careless and coherent freedom too: dance if you like, or sit talking and drinking, move around as you like, the kids running in and out, the ages of man all mixed, a six-month baby here, and Freddy from the Somme. And the interdealings seemed - perhaps it was only the music - not chaotic or quarrelsome but intriguing, richly and bravely involved, a unity whose parts were quick and differentiated. The children, for example, with bright helium balloons ran in and out among the tables and the dancers like threads of living anarchy. A room of people would never set and die so long as it had its children running wild. The balloons were a good idea. We should always have balloons, ten thousand of them, brilliant and irrepressible, on strings, lightening even further the lightness of the children.

Then Madge said: Oh, that's Mr Williams. At a table full in the midst of all the goings-on, with a drink in front of him. And that's Stan and Mavis's girl sitting next to him. And people coming up to ask him how he is. We don't want any of that, said Vic abruptly. The picture leapt. Mr Williams and his wellwishers appeared to shatter, they hurtled forward in time and when the world was recomposed he had been lost in the mêlée of dancing, drinking, chatting. Didn't know he was on it, to be honest, said Vic. Fetch him back, said Leonard in a most peculiar voice. Fetch him back this minute, do you hear? Suit yourself, said Vic. Again the world shattered, music and conversation were driven backwards, the people unsaid every word, undid every gesture in one long spasm. Bit far, said Vic. But only a moment later, as Sally's child ran past almost lifting, as it seemed, on a string of red balloons, Mr Williams reappeared, with death as plain as daylight in his face. Nice to see you, Mr Williams, a voice said. How are you feeling? Pretty well, thank you, said Mr Williams. That's the ticket, said the voice. Then a hand on his shoulder, a squeeze, it was wonderfully clear, the affectionate pressure of a married man's left hand. Mr Williams continued sitting there, the smile lapsing off his lips and his look retracting fathomlessly into holes of bone. He dabbed at his lips with a bright handkerchief. Then a woman's voice: Really lovely to see you, Mr Williams. How are you feeling? Fine, he said. A good bit better, thank you. That's the spirit, Mr Williams. And her hand came on to his, rested, departed, a beautiful hand, a bare arm, a fall of abundant blonde hair as she stooped. Should never have been there, said Betty. He wanted to, said Madge. He wrote and asked me would it be all right. He cared a lot for our Sally. Betty thought: Much good it did. Much good it did her if she got her ideas from him. Shall I freeze him? Vic asked. Vic froze Mr Williams between the efforts of his smiles, full on, in pain, lonely. Then let him go. How old was he? Betty asked. Younger than me, said Leonard. Now he was what I call ill, Vic remarked. Do you want the rest? Nobody said no. They saw it out.

Madge was upset by Vic's remark. She looked across to see how Len had taken it. Len was asking himself would it be possible to die of sadness, to be so sad that in the end, seeing no hope of any other condition, the little soul would dim to nothing and go out. Or of anxiety. To be so anxious that the head and the chest were paralysed by it and the nails clenched into the palms and stuck fast there and in that rigor mortis in the midst of life finally, imperceptibly, you passed over. Oh, you could fit the car up in the garage and end that way or find a rope and a hook or a fistful of pills, but that wasn't the thing itself, the sadness, the anxiety, actually itself doing it, the way a cancer did. And he wondered could you die of self-contempt, by being so persuaded you were unfit to live that in the end it worked, the persuasion was converted into its effect. He sat there wondering whether sadness and anxiety and self-contempt all in one, all at their worst in one, would ever without you lifting a finger be a *mortal* sickness. He thought they might, he could imagine it.

Off they go, said Vic. I like this bit. Pretty good for a first time, though I say it myself. They were leaving. See the moths in the lamplight, Vic said. Nice touch that. They were leaving, and Gwen, the day's princess, wanted all her balloons, she seemed to have gathered almost every other child's balloons, and had their leashes all together in her little fist, such a fullness and abundance of red and yellow and blue and green balloons, and there was no way they were going to get into the car with her, and hand them out or let them go, let them go up and up through the moths into the night and bump against the stars, that wasn't going to happen either. The boot, somebody said. So they lifted the lid and such fun was had by one and all getting umpteen bright balloons that only wanted to lift and be gone, getting them bundled in and held down long enough, like trying to drown something, before the lid was shut. Maybe they'll fly, maybe the car will lift off on the hill and they'll have all the lights of the towns and the motorways below.

Into the silence when they had driven off with cheers and bangings on the roof and on the boot full of balloons, into the sudden lapsing of the spirits then came the singer's voice and the piano and the trumpet and bass around her in a muted understanding. The jazz was coming through the windows of the upper room. I let it run a bit, said Vic. Ends it nicely, don't you think?

Madge was thinking of Gwen's bedroom. Just that. And the day's full routine under the rule of the chattering princess. Betty guessed as much, but thought: Count yourself lucky. I've had it all my life a room like that.

The thing ran out. Leonard opened the curtains. Not much better yet, he said. The others sat on a while. What's he do exactly, Betty asked, her new chap? He's in petrol, said Madge, not very sure. Safe at least, said Vic. We'll always need petrol. Safer than the first one anyway, said Betty. Leonard was standing facing the wall in a fashion the three on the sofa were bound to think peculiar. He had his hands in his pockets and was leaning his forehead against the wall. Madge wants a window here, he said. Don't you, Madge. His voice was hampered, stuck in his chest somewhere. Yes, said Madge. We'd get a bit more sun. Evening sun at least. I'll do it myself, Leonard said, butting gently with his forehead against the wall. I used to do things like that, you know. Didn't I put a fireplace in the other house? And what will you do, Madge? Betty asked. Get a little job somewhere. Helping out somewhere. Leonard sat down at the piano. I used to play a lot, you know. I can't read music but I can play all right. Used to be able to anyway. We know, they thought. We know. Why are you telling us things we know? Haven't touched it for years, he said. I haven't touched it since... I used to play jazz, you know. Like that chap. Funny face he had, said Betty. And his hair in a ribbon. Yes, said Leonard, like him. It used to be just like that, didn't it Madge. Yes it did, said Madge. Leonard ran the tips of his fingers along the piano lid. Then opened it.

Abduction
Shelagh Delaney

I wanted to do her in. Sitting on Manchester Piccadilly station waiting to catch the London train, I thought seriously about it. I ran through every thriller I've ever read and analysed the reasons why most of the murderers in them get caught. I reckoned that even if I did get caught it would be worth it. Capital Punishment as a deterrent was long gone, so I wouldn't risk being executed. With time off for good behaviour, plus parole, I speculated that whatever sentence I got for what was obviously a justifiable crime would eventually be cut in half. That's how I was thinking. Seriously. Can you imagine anything more inane?

Putting murder aside in the case of Ann, I contemplated other means of humiliating her and exposing her for what she was - a killer.

She didn't kill with guns, knives, blunt instruments or poison. She used money and the power of her unwavering self-assurance that she was always right.

I'm all for building confidence and self-esteem into people but, with some characters, there's a moment when confidence turns into insolence, and self-esteem transmogrifies into dangerous self-importance. What made Ann cross that line doesn't matter. She did. That's what counts. I was her older sister by six years but I can't remember her being anything but a steamrolling know-all. I used to think it was because she was fat but after the birth of my first child I got fat too. It didn't noticeably turn me into a ruthless bully. But then, as my family increased I got thinner and thinner. She didn't.

She was proud of herself and her achievements. I'm not saying she wasn't entitled to be. She was a showpiece product of the State Educational System that flourished in those 'good old days'. Like a lot of people she believed more was expected of children when she was at school. Standards were higher. Teachers were better. Family life was superior, children enjoying a kind of security tragically lacking nowadays. Being only a few years older I remembered those days too but my recollections were a bit different.

Because she loved children she trained as a doctor, specialising in paediatrics. She was good at it. She lived for her work. She only regretted that most people don't have the sense to do what she'd done when she was a young woman and get themselves sterilised.

When the best job opportunity, working in a London children's hospital, came along, she couldn't get out of Manchester quick enough. Although she'd been born and brought up there it had never been good enough. There was only one place worth living. London. When she left the only things she took from home were photographs of me and the children, her brothers and a picture of our parents on their wedding day. Otherwise it was just the clothes she stood up. She was going to make a new start and intended kitting herself out in London.

"Dont't worry about me spending money," she told her anxious mother. "What's it for?" We were all going to club together and buy her some house warming gifts but when we saw her attitude, we decided not to bother and gave her our good wishes instead.

She bought a house in Kensington, where she still lives, and soon settled down into the kind of life she had always wanted, a whirl of work, theatres, art galleries, and dinner parties.

She even took up horse riding in Hyde Park at weekends.

When she felt she'd thoroughly established herself she went back to Manchester, kidnapped her sixteen-year-old brother, and brought him with her to live in London.

He'd been born late in our parents' marriage and was much younger than she was. Getting him to go away with her wasn't hard. He'd just left school. He had no qualifications. He didn't have a job. He didn't know what kind of a job he wanted. Like most teenagers he hadn't much confidence in his mother and father and Ann, his sister, had all the answers. She also had a lovely house in London and plenty of money that she was extremely generous with. A pleasantly leafy but boring suburb of Manchester didn't stand a chance with this on offer, and more promised.

The speed and adroitness with which she had taken their son left his parents dazed in Manchester. It wasn't something they'd sat down as a family and discussed. As far as they were concerned she'd come home for a weekend visit. Her Mother had cooked all her favourite meals, much enjoyed and her father, a motor mechanic, had given her car a good going over and returned it to with clean spark plugs.

When she stood on the front doorstep of the house she'd grown up in and announced that she was taking their youngest child to London they thought she meant for a holiday and were pleased. When she put them straight about that, assuring them she was taking him to live in London, hopefully forever, their jaws dropped. She laughed and told them they looked gormless standing there with their mouths open. Promising them she could give him a better future than they could she smiled at their dumbstruck silence, told them not to worry, waved goodbye and drove away. Life in London was going to be great. No doubt about it.

Once his Father got over the abruptness of his youngest

child's leaving he was on the phone, reminding the boy that there's no such thing as a free lunch. But the boy was sixteen years old and his sister was right. Life in London was great. No doubt about it.

Soon he was enrolled in college doing media studies. He had no interest in the media. He thought he despised it. But he knew his sister expected something of him and media studies seemed the lesser of all the evils that college offered. Ann was slightly disappointed. Her sights for him had been set on accountancy or the law.

But he 'wasn't the stuff' accountants and solicitors were made of. He liked sports and music. He loved dancing. He'd learnt gardening from his father and cooking from his Mother. Because their parents were shy his older brothers had taught him everything they knew. By the time he was sixteen he'd had plenty of experience in the field of sex, drugs, smoking and drinking.

It was a wonderful life. His sister made him a generous allowance. When he over spent it she happily made up the shortfall. Her little brother, the family baby, needn't worry about money. She had plenty. She knew that money used wisely made sense. So long as everything was left in her hands everything would be all right. He laboured diligently at his media studies while ridiculing them in his heart.

Through her work as a paediatrician, Ann made friends with some very influential people. When her young brother left college they were delighted to help and found him a good job selling advertising space in *Nursing Times*. As a first job gift his sister bought him a black cashmere overcoat, six beautiful shirts, a made-to-measure suit and a briefcase. The first time he left his sister's house for the office he felt like a fool togged up in black cashmere and silk shirts. He didn't wear the coat again. He hung it in the back of his wardrobe and dumped the briefcase in a skip outside somebody's house with all the other rubbish they were clearing out, going back to the beat-up old Nike sports bag he'd brought from home and had used all through college.

Although he'd started working, his sister didn't cancel the allowance she made him every month and wouldn't accept any money for his keep at home. He realised it was time to go solo and started looking for a place of his own. While he looked he spent more and more time with his girlfriend, Marianne, who already had her own flat.

When Marianne got pregnant his sister told them to get an abortion. After the abortion she, Ann, would find him a home of his own and, if necessary, pay for it.

When they came out of shock Marianne was amazed, furious and puzzled all at the same time. How could anyone behave with such brutal insolence?

"She's more like a possessive mother than a sister," she told her him. "Are you sure you're not really her baby? Did she have you while she was still a schoolgirl and's been passing herself off as your sister ever since?"

"I've often wondered about that," he laughed. "But my brothers and eldest sister remember Mum being pregnant."

When the abortion didn't materialise and her brother and Marianne got married, Ann went from one extreme to another, and became a dangerously doting aunt. When they told her to stop lavishing presents on their daughter she told them to butt out! She'd do as she liked. Reminded that she was, after all, only the girl's aunt, not her mother and father combined, Ann simply sneered. She knew what children needed and was more aware than they were of this particular child's needs.

When this particular child's mother threw her father out because of his alcoholism, it was almost a relief to him. He'd managed to conceal his addiction for years. Marianne was the first to break his cover. For eighteen months she tried to help, but with no need for further concealment, he abandoned himself totally to the drink. He had to go.

His sister, admittedly disturbed by his heavy drinking, denied alcoholism. It was too strong a word to describe his problem. She was a doctor. Her little brother couldn't have turned into an alcholic without her noticing. The very idea! Absurd.

She welcomed him back into her Kensington home. His job with the *Nursing Times* had gone a long time ago but there was nothing to worry about. Being unemployable need not cause him anxiety. She went on giving him the allowance she'd never stopped paying into his bank account, insisting on him living rent free, providing his food, doing his laundry and even buying his clothes. He didn't want her spending so much on him. "It's only money," she'd say. "That's what it's for." She reasoned that if he had no money at all he'd steal it. She couldn't have her brother thieving to buy his booze. She'd buy it for him.

In the middle of sorting out her brother's housing and financial needs she took time to write a threatening letter to his wife. She was furious that Marianne had thrown her husband out of the family home .She told her sister-in-law she'd never considered her a fit mother. Should she, Ann, ever have cause to think that the child wasn't being brought up in a way that met with her approval she would have no hesitation in reporting Marianne to the Social Services.

When Marianne gave this letter to her husband to read he was shocked for a moment. Then he laughed and said, "Oh it's just Ann. You know what she's like. She's always over the top".

It took Ann longer to accept her brother's alcoholism than it took him. So far as she knew there had never been an alcoholic in the family. She admitted briefly, but only to herself, that apart from her immediate family the rest of her relations were a mystery to her. She had aunts, uncles and cousins she'd never met and didn't want to meet.

Mum and Dad wanted to take him home and get him better there but the great bully ball of their daughter's madness rolling over them flattened their resolve. She got him on the best rehab program money could buy. It didn't work.

He was a tender man. To see him with his wife and daughter was to see a truly loving man. When he was sober. When was he sober? He kept a record of his dry days. He was sober most of 1999. He didn't even have a drink on Millennium night when his sister's party people whose main aim was to get absolutely rat arsed before the turn of the century had surrounded him. He'd wanted to run away then, run back home to his Mother and Father. Was it possible to start all over again, he'd kept asking himself. Could he keep the beautiful bits of his life, his daughter and his wife, and dispose of the rest? Start again? Be forgiven? The words sometimes vibrated in his head. Start again. Fresh start. A clean sheet. The first day of the rest of your Life. A day at a time. I am an alcoholic. I am a recovering alcoholic. How many alcoholics can I be?

On Millennium Eve the people at his sisters party joined hands for Auld Lang Syne. Although he wanted to avoid this ritual his sister dragged him into it. As the world left one century and entered another he was crying. His sister's hopes were high. He was getting better. Back to normal. She knew how long he'd been off the booze. She'd known it would turn out all right. It was her ambition to get his daughter back for him. Convinced that with her contacts and her money she could get control. Thus she dismissed Marianne, whom he loved, as nothing, a nobody.

He was dead six weeks later. She found him sitting in a rickety old striped deckchair at the bottom of the garden. He was dressed for the cold and the leafless tree he'd chosen to sit under creaked gently above him as the wind blew. In his old Nike sports bag on the frozen grass beside him she found an opened bottle of whisky.

While he drank he'd thought about working with his father in the garden, cooking with his mother and sitting with her on the settee while they both watched *Coronation Street*. He'd remembered dancing with Marianne and how much he'd enjoyed it. He'd danced with his daughter too. They'd danced together all three of them round the flat in the kitchen, through the bathroom, the bedroom and the living room. Even in the street they'd danced. He'd smiled at the memory until his heart had stopped.

Fay and Theresa
Gwendoline Riley

The bus moved slowly through the whirling sleet. The windscreen wipers squeaked and strained back and forth, melting slushed snowflakes so that cold water streamed down constantly. Theresa, a twitchy nineteen year old red-head, was one of just a handful of passengers on that first morning trip, but she had chosen a window seat near the back and folded her coat and scarf on the seat next to her to make sure she was left alone. She had spent the journey alternately flexing her toes in her boots and tapping one foot manically. She tutted and sighed as her thoughts raced, rubbing her head against the headrest so loops of her scratchy hair worked loose of her ponytail and stood out from her head in peculiar snags and orbits. Rounding the corner into Chorlton Street, where Manchester's taller hotels and office buildings give way to the low canopies of the terminus, the bus's misted windows caught the weak rising sun, and by degrees they flared and lit up, became entirely opaque. Theresa took hold of the arms of her seat and breathed slowly. Each window was *shining*: perfect and blank.

She dragged her knee-high cardboard suitcase behind her across a pitted concourse stuck with blackened chewing gum; it bashed against bollards and thudded down steps after her. Her friend and flatmate Fay was waiting by the vending machines. A tiny little thing in a navy zip-up coat and jeans cut off just above the ankles to reveal slumped socks above tide marked baseball boots, she was bundled up in a green scarf and gloves, her dark hair tucked into a yellow and black striped hat. She let her cat-eye glasses hang from her ears like a chinstrap, closing one eye at a time to stare into a cup of coffee she'd bought more to warm her hands on than to drink. Theresa stood in front of her for fully a minute before her friend was aware of her, pushed her glasses back up her nose and looked at her.

Theresa is double jointed in her left elbow and so when she stands, as she was doing then, with her hands jammed in her hip pockets, one arm looks like it's bended the wrong way. In summer, in short sleeves, it looks more dramatic, the sheeny skin inside the joint stretches and shows up a lattice of red thread veins deep below, but even in a thick winter coat it's an unsettling trick, a limb jabbing out at such an odd angle.

"Stop doing that with your arm," Fay said, and took hold of her friend's elbow and clicked it back into place.

"You look disappointingly familiar," she said.

"Don't be deceived," Theresa said, picking up her case properly, but making no move to leave, "I have a Tweetie-Pie and a Coca-Cola bottle tattooed on my ass."

Fay leant back against the wall and twitched her eyebrows, her lips twitched too: a suppressed smile. "On your what?" She said and held her friend's gaze. "Come on, car's this way."

They drove home in silence. Theresa sat listening to the changing tones of the tyres on the wet roads, watching with one open eye the monochrome early morning suburbs scrolling by.

"So you know what I'm going to ask," she said, without looking at Fay, who in turn did not miss a beat when she answered, while peering up into the mirror,

"I've not seen him."

By the time they got home bright sunlight was hitting the snow on the car bonnets and the bin lids. Dew was still stuck like jewellery tears on the black twigs of the leafless tree in front of their squat concrete block in Salford. The path to the porch was frozen over with packed ice. There was no way around it. Even the strip of barren soil by the fence was glazed and afforded no purchase. Theresa slid her case across to the door; it spun slowly towards the step, making a thin, scratching sound. She started to pick her way after it, taking baby steps and holding her arms out: her hands balled in tight fists, her eyes wide in anticipation of slamming into the ground with her knees, her palms, her backside. Fay walked alongside carefully; her rubber-soled shoes offering more grip than the knee high pointed boots Theresa wore under Levi's rolled halfway up her calf. When Theresa thought she was going to slip she reached out and took hold of Fay's scarf. She righted herself but Fay teetered for a moment.

"If you're going to fall *on your ass*, I think we should do this independently," she said.

"Yes." Theresa said, taking hold of her friend's sleeve, "Independently while grabbing onto each other."

*

Theresa unlocked her bedroom and took her suitcase inside; opened it on the floor and found a tape amongst the tangle of jeans and cardigans. She clicked it into the player on the dresser, then lay down on her bed with her hands behind her head and her wool coat and pointy boots still on. There was a tapping on the door; a green door gripped by the brass knuckles of a series of locks.

"It's open," she said.

Fay came in and leant against the doorframe, looking around the small room she hadn't seen for three months. She'd pulled the jack leads out from the back of her turntable and speakers and tied them round the top of her jeans. She stood in the doorway and jerked her hipless middle side to side so the plugs swung neatly.

"Sound tech. chic," she said, and smiled.

Theresa raised her eyebrows but didn't reply. She sucked on a ratty snatch of her red hair and resumed staring into a corner of the ceiling. Fay climbed over the towers of taped up cardboard boxes, from the time when Theresa thought she might leave for good. Boxes she would now have to get round to unpacking again.

"How's your gran?"

With a jerk of her hips Theresa flipped over to lie on her front, and looked at Fay with one eye while rubbing the other one.

"Okay. Glad to see the back of me I think." She yawned. "I bought you a present; it's on top of the case, in the tissue paper..."

It was a cheap snow-globe. The yellow cab and cop car were stupidly big next to the plastic skyscrapers. Fay nodded and turned it upside down a couple of times, but the liquid inside wasn't viscous enough, so no matter how hard you shook it the snow fell too fast and was almost instantly back on the bottom; the sealed-up scene as static and lifeless as before.

"Cheers," she said.

Theresa blew on her cold hands.

"I'll put the heating on now. They fixed it at last," Fay said. "Do you want a cup of tea?"

Theresa thought about it.

"Ok, thanks. But don't put any milk in. I can't digest that substance anymore."

She got under her duvet, pulled it tight over her head, then set about prising her cigarettes and lighter from her jeans pocket.

A minute or so later she heard Fay come in and put a mug

on the bookcase. She waited another five minutes until she heard her leave, then got up and twitched the curtain to watch her friend edge down the path, get in her car and finally drive off to the cafe bar in town where she worked days and where Theresa used to work nights. Then she had a stretch and a yawn and took her mug into the kitchen to find some milk, and some ginger biscuits. But the biscuit tasted of nothing to her: it was just dry and powdery. She spat it out: a beige clod in the empty sink, then took her tea back to her bedroom. In her suitcase she found a long letter Fay had written her while she was away. Its six pages had been unfolded and folded in coffee houses all up and down Avenue A, and although it was franked with cup rings, she'd never been able to really process its meaning: the a's had yawned at her, the o's gaped, the e's grinned horribly. Theresa had looked at it for hours, taking nothing in. There were too many damn exclamation marks; a blizzard of phoney punctuation, she couldn't connect the sentiments with her taciturn old friend. She put the letter in the top drawer of her dresser, and unpacked some clothes on top of it.

*

Dean had moved in to the flat directly above Fay and Theresa in September. Theresa would sit down in the freezing darkness of the stairwell with her elbows on her knees and listen to him strumming and screaming at all hours. She felt like he was singing all her secrets. But it was Fay who spoke to him first, when they were on the same late bus back from town. She sat on the edge of Theresa's bed to tell her about it, whispering, *You'll never guess who I just met?*

"And he was awkward. He kept jutting his chin out and nodding too much. I think he's really a shy guy," she said, "The kind of guy who never dances."

Theresa shrugged. "That wouldn't be shyness, that would be vanity. I bet he dances, but maybe not in public. In the kitchen like me." Theresa smiled in the dark.

She had only seen him from her window, walking to or from the shop or the bus stop. He had short dark hair, and broad shoulders which he always seemed to be twitching, like he was arguing with himself in his mind. She found him formidable, because she fancied him a lot, but when she summoned the courage to smile at him, one evening on her way home from college, he smiled back.

"That's a good look," he said, leaning on the gatepost and looking her up and down. She was wearing her folded up jeans, and pointy boots, and a grey twinset.

"Kind of snowbound, Mid-west, 1950s, *In Cold Blood...*"

She stopped in the driveway and folded her arms "Yeah, that's what I was going for."

He looked right at her, "You have a 1950s figure," he said.

"I know. It's completely unfashionable...but there you go."

"It's great."

"It's okay."

'It makes me think of.... slide guitar and...motels and ...""

"Serial murder."

"For sure."

Theresa jerked her chin up and waited for him to make a move to leave or go inside, or say something else. But it seemed he was happy hanging out by the gatepost. She folded her arms tighter, then grinned at her shoes and kicked some leaves about a bit.

'Well..." She nodded. "See you, I guess. .."

"I guess," he said. Then, "Anyway, you should come up sometime. Few drinks, few laughs..." He twitched his shoulders and kicked at the gatepost. "Anytime, I'm never really busy."

114

"Okay." She said and went inside.

That evening they sat on opposite ends of his sagging settee smoking his clove cigarettes and talking seriously. Dean had a voice like a cello that's out of tune. He spoke like he sang: with this shudder, as if he was crushing his Megarider in his pocket and trying not to grind his jaw. It was a voice made to pronounce words like *suffering* and *bullshit*. Even the way he breathed was effortful; sounded thick lipped, snot-nosed and tantrum prone. But at least, Theresa thought, he was sincerely trying to communicate when he spoke. Too often a person's biliousness evanesces into a haughty, calm cordiality. There's nothing more repellent. Then they hate everything quietly, and with an utter lack of conviction. Those are the people who get shark eyes when they're drunk, suddenly looking at you with these hole-punched expressionless voids. Dean and Theresa got through a bottle of gin between them that night but didn't get maudlin or silly. His whole demeanour was like pinching a feather spine and brushing it backwards, but he had a kind of gravitas about him, Theresa thought, even when pulling at the neck of his T-shirt or kicking the skirting board.

When she said she'd better go back downstairs he said,

"Theresa, do you reckon it would be all right if I kissed you?"

She widened her eyes and looked at her knees, then nodded okay. He leant over, and afterwards he turned his mouth down at the corners and said,

"I've been building up to that."

He slid up to the centre seat on the settee and put an awkward arm around her. They both stared ahead and she wanted to laugh but didn't. She turned and put both arms round his neck and then it was him who laughed.

Later on he held her hand across the kitchen table while their toast was toasting.

*

Dean came downstairs the next day while Fay was at work. They listened to some records in Theresa's bedroom. By half four it was getting dark outside, and the light from the paper-shaded lamp seemed to be painting the white walls a nasty yellow, so Theresa clicked it off and let the bluish twilight spill through the tangle of bare twigs in her window. She locked the door too, and when Fay came back at six and called out to her, she held her hand over Dean's mouth, and so it was in complete silence that he ran his fingers over the silverish slice scars on her left forearm; the cat stripe stretch marks swagging the tops of her thighs: both these things looked to him like the rents in the dull clouds where the white winter sun glows through. Theresa turned away and curled up, her heart thudding dully. She didn't know what to do and she didn't want to look into his eyes. He ran his fingers over the stubble on her shins, then slipped an icy arm around her middle, spread his fingers over her tiny doughy stomach, then moved it up to the cockleshell ridges of her ribs. He whispered in her ear. "Turn round," he said. But it took her a little while to do that. And later when she looked down at the squash of her thigh against his lean, slippy stomach she felt something like dread.

All the next day she had an obscure restlessness working inside her. It felt to her like the luminous something you can see in storm clouds sometimes. When the day's been dark, and you can't wait, *cannot wait* for it to break. When the weather was like that she could never stay indoors. She had to go out and see the sky amber, dark and light at the same time, flashing. Then in a beat the raindrops shattering everywhere, making tiny glassy sculptures on the pavements. She didn't know what it meant. She knocked on at Dean's in the afternoon, when she got in from college. He answered the door in his boxers and a T-shirt, kissed her cheek on the doorstep and then she followed him inside. There was a cup of tea on the floor, a blanket crumpled up on one end of the settee, and a book resting open on it like a pitched roof. He offered her a drink, she said no, then he sat down next to her and leant forward, asking about her day. She answered his questions in monosyllables. She could feel silence howling all around them. She wanted to smile but she couldn't. Wanted to talk like they had before but couldn't. She knew the words ready in her mouth would be taken downstairs again, unsaid. Eventually the alert look left his face and he frowned and slumped back in his seat, started flicking the channels on the remote control.

So she just said she was tired, went back to her flat early, drew the curtains tight in her room, and waited until it was time to go into work. She lay back with her ankles crossed and her arms folded and stared at the ceiling. Later on she watched the portable TV at the bottom of her bed. With the volume turned right down and the colour muted to an unobtrusive glow, it was a small, grubby, window on the world.

She watched exhilarated eyewitnesses shake their heads and gesticulate with gloved hands; their hair blowing in their faces; the fires raging behind them. She pointed her big toe to switch channels, to a game show, with a glamorous girl turning lit letter blocks around to form a catchphrase. Those half hidden sentences sometimes held a mistaken meaning for her, for a split second. She tried to follow as best she could. But in the moments when the screen blanked after the ad-breaks the room was silent and almost dark. Then she really started to panic, looking across at his belt threaded through the handle of her wardrobe door, the mirror he'd scruffed his hair in. She drew her legs up, squeezed her eyes shut and dug her teeth into her knees. She breathed slowly and made herself calm down.

It was a fortnight before she spoke to him again, when an impulse made her skip the afternoon at college and go home early. Dean wasn't in, so she went to put her bag in the flat before sitting on his step to wait for him. She'd barely opened the front door before she heard something wrong. A sound which seemed to shine through Fay's shut bedroom door, shine through the cracks with an awful supernatural light. A noise she didn't understand. Theresa walked towards it. She put her bag between her feet, then sat down against the small radiator in the dark hallway. The cold metal stung through her cardigan. As she listened, her face was entirely vacant: her eyes blinking fast like insect wings, automatic and un-decorative, her smile bland. She wasn't really concentrating to maintain this serenity - it was more like a decision had been made, *just for a few minutes*, she'd thought, and let herself leave, her mouth twitching with an almost giggle as she felt the substance of herself vaporising into a cool calm mist. She held a hand out and imagined herself blurring around the edges. Other images had flashed vaguely in the back of her mind: her friend's little grippy hands moving up and down his back...her mouth on his neck.... rubbing her child legs together like tinder. Theresa just kept on smiling. When they came out she was smiling still.

*

Theresa walked round to the off licence, she stole a pair of Fay's shoes so she wouldn't slip over on the way. On the way back she caught the eye of a kid sitting in the back of a car: belted in, staring out, he looked at her with no expression on his face. She stared back. She felt sick. She spent the afternoon drinking in the kitchen chair. When Fay got home there was a bottle in the bin, a mug in the sink, and her friend was sprawled out on the counter. On her limp left hand was written in Biro DON'T GO OUT. When she groaned and sat up Fay saw that this sentiment was echoed in a pale print on her right cheek.

Fay sat down on the other chair and looked out of the window for a few minutes.

"You *should* come out, everyone's been asking after you today."

Theresa shrugged.

"I wish you'd been here on New Year's Eve," Fay said. "It was a pathetic tragedy. I thought it would be cool to drink out of a pineapple all night. So I spent the afternoon in here, hollowing out this pineapple and laughing to myself. But I didn't realise that after two drinks it goes kind of waterlogged and soggy. So at the end of the party I was in the kitchen drinking beer out of this collapsed pineapple. I was all sticky. The next day everyone was saying, "What were you doing? You're disgusting, Where's your self-respect?"... 'Cause I was sick as well. Sick all down myself..."

"I get the picture...." Theresa sighed and stared at her, "So why did you do it?"

There was a long pause before Fay answered. "I was bored, I suppose, didn't know how it would turn out...was lonely." She turned her little hands palm up.

"You were lonely. That's the worst possible excuse for anything."

"You think?"

"Yeah I do. And by the way, Fay," here Theresa took a deep and luxuriant breath, "I feel so lonely that I just want to *howl*. So..."

Fay leant back in her chair and looked at her friend then down at her forearm, which she scratched. Then they both watched through the window the old man from across the street come out of his house and drop a carrier bag of rubbish in his bin before getting into his red car and driving off.

"When I was a teenager," Fay said, taking her cat-eye glasses off and polishing them on her jumper, "I always carried a copy of *Howl* about with me. Everywhere I went. A battered old hardback copy that my..."

"What?" Theresa threw up her hands.

"What?" Fay grinned and widened her eyes.

"Is this a conversation or a word association game?" Theresa stood up, "Jesus."

Fay stared up,

"Christ," she said and laughed to herself, "and now I've talked myself into a verbal cul-de-sac..."

Theresa nodded and sucked air through her teeth, still staring out of the window.

".... and then *leapt* behind a privet." She said, "Pineapple indeed."

Theresa took the snow-globe off the windowsill and turned it upside down.

One evening while she was away Theresa had walked uptown and sat down in a park facing the East River. The old man on the other end of her bench wasn't dressed for the weather: he was head to toe in white sports gear: plimsolls, knee socks, shorts and a polo shirt. His stout legs were glossy, brown, hairless. His face was ancient and his eyes were milky. He called her 'miss' and himself 'the General' and when he found she was new in town he pointed out everything on the skyline: the Triborough Bridge, the Hell's Gate Bridge, Roosevelt Island, Ward Island, Shea Stadium...

"And up there's heaven," he said and looked up at the clear night sky. The girl sitting at the next bench along had looked up too. But Theresa hadn't.

Going To The Dogs
Wayne Clews

Vince, 32.

Vince was an industrial cleaner from Ordsall who picked up trodden-in chewing gum from the carpets of HMV with one of those big hoovers. When he picked me up, I was technically unconscious, sprawled in the corner of a club with my laces undone. As I left with him, I did blearily wonder who he was, but he seemed to be in charge so I meekly shuffled after him and left my coat in the cloakroom. He lived in a high rise with only a few books including a DIY manual he clearly hadn't opened. He put a porn film on that I could barely see and he undressed me. We had uncomfortable sex on the sofa as I lapsed in and out of sleep. In the morning he drove me home in his cleaner's van on his way to work in Birmingham. I made him drop me on the main road so that I didn't have far to walk to the newsagent's for fags. But he pulled up there himself and I was forced to hide behind the bus shelter in the rain. He did a U-turn and drove straight past me so that I would have been painfully visible, hunched and damp against an advert for shampoo. That's a funny way to go to Birmingham, I thought, and went to buy my fags. My coat turned up on Tuesday night.

Paul, 26.

Paul told me he was a student and I think I muttered something disparaging about my experience of mature students but he was incredibly tall and I don't think he heard me. He already had that closely cropped hairstyle of a man going inevitably bald. I did my usual trick of getting very drunk and ended up at his flat anyway. His house-mate gave me a needling glance when I demanded a drink and clearly thought me unworthy. I exchanged phone numbers with Paul in the morning but I couldn't read his and mine was a false one, just one digit incorrect. It turned out he was in a choir and they did a concert the following Christmas where I was working temporarily. A colleague, who I had never liked, pointed him out and said he was sure he had slept with him too and Paul had wet the bed in the night. He mentioned Paul's red futon so it must have been the same man. I hadn't thought to check the mattress after my stay so I just hid behind the till and Christmas novelties.

Ray, 35.
Ray had hounded me all night in a dreary club. I was interminably rude to him, made him buy drinks then wandered off to find my friend who was in the midst of an illicit affair. When 2am arrived and the lights came up, Ray confronted me again. "Did you find anyone better?" he asked with such awful hopefulness that I felt obliged to go through with it all but refused to walk up the steps out of the club with him lest anyone should see. He wouldn't get a taxi so I assumed he must be poor and traipsed after him whining, "How much further?" like a disconsolate toddler. To entertain me he began a debate about bike lights as someone cycled past. Which did I prefer, he wondered, the ones that stayed on constantly or the ones that flashed as you pedalled? He preferred the latter and I said I had little opinion on the subject but would welcome his thoughts on the Middle East crisis. Sex was mercifully brief but he insisted I stay and, since I had no idea where I was, I did. In the morning I awoke uncomfortably to find Ray already inside me. I lay there and pretended to sleep until he finished, then I got dressed. He wittered on about tea and wrote

his number on a large piece of paper, forcing that upon me too. I caught a bus from outside his flat in the wrong direction and it took hours to get home.

Andy, 19.

Being so young, Andy only wanted to talk and the bar was so loud that we came back to mine and I opened a cheap bottle of wine which he didn't like. At first we only talked about the parlous state of my CD collection (half he hated, half he had never heard of) and then he revealed that he was in the armed forces and had never done anything like this before. I felt a little unnerved but he stayed the night anyway. When I kissed him, he cried and said he just wanted to be held by someone. In the morning, his mother rang his mobile and demanded to know where he had disappeared to last night. I dropped him at Victoria Station.

Rob, 33.

I don't know where I met Rob. I had stormed out of a party after a row about something I forget and suspect I met him on the street. As we walked to his house, he revealed he had just got out of prison for armed robbery. I asked him if he was going to kill me but he didn't rightly reply. He had been housed by the council on a virtually burnt-out estate and had no bed. On the walls were pictures of boxers that he had drawn whilst inside. I reflected on how stupid I was being as I drank a can of Kestrel but later Rob couldn't get it up so we just went to sleep on cushions from the sofa spread out on the floor. He only had one sleeping bag and gave that to me, he slept under his coat. In the morning I made a hasty exit. He pointed directions, nude, from his front door until one of his neighbours wandered past and, with a cheery "Hello!" took in the full incriminating scene. I didn't listen to his directions properly but eventually found the city centre. On the bus home, I thought that Rob's life would be murder round there anyway now.

Ugly Man, 50.

I never intended this. I was in Belle Vue so I must really have been going to the dogs. The pints I had drank before my bus journey had caught up with me so I went into the public toilets with only the purest intentions. There was a man in there with a carrier bag at his feet already at the urinal. I took the vacant spot and under his gaze was unable to pee. He was frenetically masturbating with little visible result and it was then that he hissed an offer of a tenner if he could wank me off. I was short of cash and the man looked so lonely and impotent that I nodded and allowed him, taking the money first, like a proper pro. When I came, he caught it all in his hand, presumably for some nefarious purposes of his own. I left without ever having that pee.

Outside, in the evening sun, I walked a few yards before I felt a chill sweat lace my skin. I clutched onto some railings and thought I was going to be sick, but the moment passed.

Kirsten vs The City
Clare Pollard

It has been two months since Kirsten Woolly moved to
the city, and her days have begun to settle into a routine. Fear is
part of the day. Fear that brings blood in the ears and a bass-line
heart. Fear that cling-films her in sweat and shows horror-movies
in her head:

Tonight, Kirsten Woolly IS
The Mad Knife-Man's Victim!
Directed by: her paranoia.

However, she has got used to this, just as she has grown
accustomed to the rest of her day and – for now at least – she
doesn't worry about that walk home until she has climbed off the
bus at the top of that dark, narrow street.

Her days generally go like this:
8.00 - Wake up to local radio and the traffic report
(congestion: *everywhere*)
8.30 - Catch the 8.00 bus to work. Agitate hangover by
having to stand, and wobbling a lot, as it crawls – slow
as a carnival float – past the same stale chain stores that
every high street has, as if by Xerox.
9.00 - Late for work. Grab a skinny almond latte, even
though she doesn't strictly like coffee – finds it, to be

frank, a little acrid – but rather likes the associations (hip young people discussing relation ships, biscotti, big funky cups.) Also, on non-dieting days, a pain au raisin.

9.05 - Check e-mail, which will be crammed with adverts for fake degree certificates and porn, and fwds from the two chick-lit loving girls in the office, Kelly and Joanne, entitled '10 reasons why chocolate is better than men!' or 'A quick guide to learning lad-speak.'

9.20-1.00 - Have shit time in shit job doing boring shitty things.

1.00-1.30 - Lunch. Generally a sandwich from the shop across the road that sounds unspeakably exotic (Crayfish, roquette and lemon; Aromatic duck; Scotch beef with parmesan and onion relish) but tastes like...well, bread mainly. And cheap margarine.

1.30-6.00- More shit.

6.00 - Queue for bus in endless, soul destroying rain.

6.30 – Bus.

7.00 – Arrive at the top of that dark, narrow street.

The street is lit badly, by two flushed, flickering streetlights. The pavement is puddled. Kirsten Woolly usually sings to herself as she walks down it, or hums, she's a big hummer: hmm-hmm hm hm hmmmmm... A second, non-singing voice in her head usually says: *shit, shit, you should have got a taxi you stupid bitch, never mind the money. Money doesn't matter if you're DEAD.* She jumps like a firecracker when she hears noises, and glances repeatedly over her shoulder to check there's no one there. If there is someone there, she hopes that it's a) a woman or b) actually two people, completely unrelated, one thus acting as a safety guard and potential witness. If there is a lone man, her skin will suddenly feel thrilled and awful, and she will concentrate on her breathing, and hug herself tighter, and, often get her keys out of her pocket and lodge them between her knuckles with the sharp bit sticking out as a makeshift weapon. By this point her inner voice will probably be alternating between: *go for the bollocks or earring* and *you wet fucking blanket* and *ohmygodohmygodohmygod*. So far she has not been attacked. It is a ten minute walk. Then home.

Ah! Home. A city-centre flat with ants, damp, unpredictable heating and light-switches blackened by the fingerprints of former tenants. Kirsten lives there with her boyfriend, Sam, and one of the pros of this is that he's always in when she gets home to make her a cup of tea, and reassure her that she's safe. Sam exudes 'safe.' The flat, unfortunately - despite the false burglar alarm he knocked up for the front, blue and white with a stripe and the name: SECURITOR, which he thought up himself – is pretty much an everything-must-go grand giveaway for anyone who bothers to push lightly on the bathroom window, where the frame has rotten away. Also, Kirsten lies awake worrying about arson. Their road is so fully parked with burnt-out cars, it is though they gravitate towards it in death, like an elephant's graveyard. At least a couple of times a week, Sam will glance out and see a couple of kids have set fire to a wheelie bin or skip, and dial 999 without even bothering to pass comment. Sometimes, in bed, as he snores open-mouthed, his arm still round her from their earlier sexless, brother-sister embraces, a police siren hollering outside, Kirsten will think she smells smoke, and jolt upright with terror. OK, so you could say that 9 out of 10 times she probably *does* smell smoke, but still – I would pinpoint this as the beginning.

The beginning of what? Of the madness, of course. Did I not tell you? This city breaks people.

What city is this? It is a city like any other: sprawling, dirty, busy, overpopulated, riddled with muggings and pigeons, with a wide choice of cinemas, theatres, clubs and multicultural restaurants. A city with not enough hospitals and too many drug deals, with homelessness and holy places, squares and ghettos, high-rises and penthouses, unimaginable wealth and poverty.

It is a city like any other: a place that humans are not made to endure. A place for which we have not evolved. A place of sin and squalor and loneliness and artifice and head-hurting choice and pollution and traffic. A place all our genes scream out against. A filthy zoo, in which we cage ourselves.

Don't get me wrong, I love the city, so does Kirsten.

But this city breaks people.

So, where were we? Oh, the beginning. Kirsten Woolly is walking home after a particularly shit day at the office, looking forward to the chicken pie Sam has txted her to say is in the oven. Sam is a good cook, particularly when it comes to really boring, laborious things like making a white or hollandaise sauce, shortcrust pastry, Yorkshire puddings etc. Kirsten is not particularly afraid on this evening, as there is a middle-aged couple walking approximately ten metres ahead of her, and there is safety in numbers. It is drizzling. A FOR SALE sign flaps in a gust. The rain has lulled, briefly, but she can still hear rain dripping from the gutters, and it takes a minute for her to notice another sound, beneath this: the sound of footsteps. Kirsten turns and looks back, but cannot see anyone. She walks on. The footsteps pick up, getting closer and closer - hollow wet-sounding stomps. She looks back again and there is still no one, just wind-shaky shadows and a gingerbread fox. A sudden, frightening thought grabs her: what if they're hiding deliberately? What if it's a stalker? After a couple of moments, she dismisses this as obsessive, and hurries nearer to the couple, sticking close until she gets to her door. Ah! Home. Safety. Sam is stood by the bin in the kitchen, peeling a carrot. "Nice day?"

"Yep," she lies, taking off her coat. "How was yours?"

"Fine. It was nice at the staff meeting today – I really felt that the company's beginning to *cohere* around a shared set of ideals." He looks over at her and grimaces. "You're wet, aren't you? You better have a vitamin C tablet."

"Yeah," she says, suddenly overwhelming bored by the thought of another night in. Moving in with Sam was impelled by economic pressure, really. Oh, she likes him – what's not to like? He's loyal, kind, reliable... But who is she kidding? The cons are starting to add up:

> He keeps saying he's 'there for her' (yeah, yeah – well meant but very annoying)
> He is interested in the ISAs and bond referrals, and knows the interest rates of most major banks.
> His jumpers.
> He doesn't like any position apart from missionary/girl-on-top as he apparently can't cum unless he's looking into a woman's eyes, and thinks doggy-style (Kirsten's favourite) is 'degrading' for her.
> Argyle socks.
> Keen interest in golf.

On the pro side, he is:

> Very good-looking, in a cheesy, blonde sort of way.
> Good at massage.
> Always 'there for her' (yeah, yeah – she slags it off, but it's quite good during her period when she wants him to

cycle a mile in the rain for wine and a video.)

Anyway, anyway. Kirsten's moved in with him now, so she's determined to give him a chance. And is doing. The fact that she's started to drink a bottle of chardonnay every night she stays in with him isn't *necessarily* a sign that they're doomed. She glances through the TV guide. "People who want to be famous, slags on holiday or 'I love last month?'" she asks.

"There's a show on the history channel, actually, about the first ever case of share fraud and the South Sea bubble…"

"Oh," Kirsten answers. It seems the only adequate answer, accurately summing up the sheer weight of her underwhelmedness. She thinks about those footsteps.

At night, they tap-tap through her dreams.

The footsteps follow her home the next night. And the next night. Kirsten Woolly's fear mounts. On the third night, she decides to get a cab home, and sod the cost. It is a black cab that smells ill with citrus air-freshener, as though lemons have been farting. The driver, a short, brutish man with a piggy nose, is quick to tell her that he believes paedophiles should be nailed up by their cocks in front of Buckingham Palace, but otherwise seems harmless. Or at least, does, until he turns off the usual route. Kirsten's heart thuds: *de-dud de-dud de-dud* as they go deeper into where-the-fuck, and then she catches his eyes in the mirror. They seem to be laughing. God! No! Her Stalker, disguised cunningly as a taxi driver! In a quick, clumsy move, she leaps to the door, opens it, and tumbles out onto the street.

As she runs away, past a Chinese restaurant laden with delicate paper lanterns, past a row of Georgian terraces, past a tramp asleep on a bench, she hears his faint voice yell: "Seven pounds you little bitch!"

The city. Can you hear it? At night, unable to sleep, Kirsten can hear nothing else. The faint screams of prostitutes demanding their money. Motorbikes parking outside 24-hr garages for fags and pasties. Clubbing. Glassings. The keening wails of ambulances. Can you hear the rats, scrabbling and swimming beneath you, *squeak-squeak!* Millions of them, sick-blooded, crawling clawingly towards the dark heart of the city. Can you hear the foxes turn over the bins, and feast on pigeon corpse, yesterdays' cat-curry, junk food, remnants of ready-meals for one. Can you hear the shots? Can you hear the money? Can you hear the street cleaner's chugging across the square, spraying vomit off steps? Can you hear the footsteps? Can you hear the starlessness? Can you hear the fear?

Sam agrees to meet Kirsten after work every day, so they can go home together. This means she has to hang around the office longer than she'd like, but at least it's brownie points with the boss. Sam's condition is that she goes to the doctor, and as he's being so 'there for her' Kirsten agrees, and gets put on a course of anti-depressants: *Lustral.* For a while, the fear seems to subside.

It is now Friday, and for the first night since she bolted the taxi, Kirsten is in on her own. She has double-locked the door. She is adding pesto to her baked beans to make them feel more luxurious. When it is ready she takes it to their bedroom a tray, and eats off her lap whilst watching an aspirational TV chef. They are deep-frying Bounty bars, whilst their friends are saying: "It's all our birthdays rolled into one," and pulling cum-faces. Kirsten is fascinated by cum-faces. On public transport she finds it amusing to imagine the men sat opposite her ejaculating –

whether they look very serious, like newscasters breaking a story about floods in India, or like they've just dropped a kettle on their foot. She is just finishing the final sweet, slippery gobful of beans when she hears a clunking in the kitchen; a clatter of fragments of cup or plate. Feels her heart in her chest, like some alien object, and panic quivering through her sinews. "Sometimes only trashy food will do," the TV chef coos, and Kirsten thinks *shit, shit, shit*, because this is her worst fear, the very worst thing, and it is happening, *now*.

    As soon as she hears the clatter Kirsten gets under the duvet and covers her face. It is pure instinct, this sense that if she cannot see them they will not have to kill her: she will not have to be fucked and slit all over the brash floral bedspread, which she bought with Sam on some dull, middle-aged Sunday in Ikea. Sam loves DIY, and views Ikea as some sort of Disney World for grown ups, cramming his big blue bag excitedly with door hooks, plastic bag dispensers and more shot glasses than anyone could ever conceivably need. Or worse, saying repeatedly: "Well, why not, it's only *x* pounds," in some awful devil-may-care way that's subtext is *you only live once*. The duvet has a creamy, pissy smell of insomnia and sex. It makes everything seem unreal, like a film she's too wet to watch. A horror film:

Tonight, Kirsten Woolly IS
Brutally Raped in her own Home!
Directed by: cruel, cruel fate.

    Perhaps – she tells herself, desperately - the footsteps on the stairs are actually the central heating making that noise it does sometimes, or a mouse behind the cooker, and this is just a nightmare she will wake from, or has already woken from. But then the truth winds Kirsten again, and her hands begin to tremble like an alcoholic's; her eyes becoming hot and fresh with wetness. It is airless under the duvet, the light is like a fever. She lets out a small fart that smells of beans, then worries that they've heard, or maybe that's good and they'll go away.

Kirsten crouches like this for ten minutes, drinking sweat off her lip. Jolting at each noise as though she's popping out of a toaster. Her body cowers in a permanent flinch at the thought of fists, knives...guns. Shit, they could have guns. At last she hears them enter her room. Something hard butts into her left bum-cheek, and she thinks: knife, cock, gun, in that order. "Who the fuck's this? I thought you fucking said they were out," a voice says.

"Well, I made a fucking mistake."

"Well, what the fuck do we do now?"

"Excuse me," Kirsten recites, from the script she has perfected over the last five minutes, her voice thin and panty. "I haven't seen you, I can't tell the police anything. Just please, please, take everything you want and go." She hears a soft *sssss* of piss; one of them is pissing on the carpet.

"Nice computer you got," he says. "Rich bitch are you?"

"No – I –"

"I say we just stab her," he continues. "Fuck her up her rich little arse with a knife." There is a moment when Kirsten knows she will die, and wishes it were already done. She feels the hard thing, again, at the back of her neck, and it is definitely a knife. Her body buckles with a sob of agony, the anticipated pain so great it is as though it has begun. And then there is a laugh, and doors slamming. When Sam arrives back, two hours later, he finds her still under the covers.

She screams as he draws them back.

Oh, did I not tell you? There were no burglars.

Sam makes her a brew and reassures her, repeatedly, that

137

the house is untouched, the bathroom window still in place. If you can call it reassurance. In a way it scares her more. In bed she clings to him, desperately, unable to sleep, petrified of mental breakdown (schizochondria?) The next day, every time she hears a kid yelling on the street – say: "Kick it over here!" or "Whassup!" – her reaction is to question: is this voice external or is it *in my head?* She is on the edge of…what? Being sectioned? Suicide? Being pointed at in the street?

No, *worse.*

This city breaks people.

Kirsten Woolly goes for a curry with the girls from work, pre-arranged weeks before. Prawn saag and a naan with coconut. There is a carousel of accompaniments: a candy-sweet mango chutney, raita that smells of face-pack, a snot-loosening lime pickle. Kelly and Joanne spend most of the meal debating the Big Question - why can't men commit? – and saying how *weird* it is how quickly they've got tipsy. Kirsten has a brief, scary moment of wondering if the rendition of Robbie Williams' 'Millennium' she can hear in the background is actually *all in her mind*, but otherwise copes fairly well. Whilst blocking out one of Kelly's particularly dull anecdotes about following the same diet as J-Lo and getting green pee, she even makes some resolutions to put her life back on track. Things will be fine, Kirsten decides, so long as she gets out of London for more long weekends, buys a rape alarm and – most important, this – dumps Sam. Yep, she realises that more than anything what's been really stressing her out is the fact she's moved in with him and doesn't actually *fancy* him anymore. It has to be done. Then maybe she can move into a new place, more accessible, on a better lit street and ta-da! Life solved. She doesn't want to give in: to pack up and leave the city. She has wanted to live here since she was a small girl, lured by the juicy kitsch of neon, the gritty cartoon bubble-lettering of graffiti, the library with its sun-bleached dome of books, the exuberance of the flower market, the cool kids in the square, the rock and roll legends, the famous bars, the famous residents. The packed sizzling kebabs, pocketed with chilli sauce, purchasable on every corner. She won't give in. Instead she'll give up on Sam.

It sounds simple.

But Kirsten is underestimating the city. The city that is breathing all around her as it speaks. The city with its haunted rooms, its buried rivers, its secrets, its skeletons, its blood-soaked earth. The city that stands on plague pits, massacres, graveyards, pogroms. The suicides beneath the crossroads; the curses laid on the roofs. Nothing is simple in cities: they are huge, messy complex systems, riddled with coincidence, flaws, fluke, chance, romance, tragedy.

Kirsten underestimates the city's spell on her. The time she saw a transvestite cracking the head of a small man with her heel; all those posters: *Did you see an incident here…?* by taped off areas. The flasher in the park. The urban myths. They are all in her head.

She is haunted by the city.

She is haunted like the city.

When the cash till eats her card, Kirsten Woolly realises she will have to get the bus home and make that walk. But it's okay, it's fine, she feels emboldened by alcohol. In fact, since the robbery-that-never was, she has decided those footsteps were probably all in her mind. Now she determines to beat them. When she climbs out at the end of that dark, narrow street, she feels reasonably proud and bolshy. And she's fine. She's fine walking past the FOR SALE sign, the sleeping tramp with his 2-litre bottle of cider, the cars with their smashed windows and gaping absences near the dashboard, the daubed insults to the world on brick, - Fuck you all! – the glutted bins with their honeyed smell, the needles, the windows bright with early Christmas lights and injection-moulded Santas. She's fine, really, until…

The footsteps. Those hollow, wet-sounding stomps. She looks back and there is nothing but an airborne plastic bag. A helicopter rumbles overhead, searching for some escapee. She puts her foot in a poo. "Shit! Shit!" Still no sound. In her anger she yells out: "Who is it? Show your bastard cowardly face!" Nothing.

Ok, ok, so it's in her head. Fine then, she can control it, she can stop it. She finds herself remembering a move they showed her once at youth club: make your hand into a weird, two-pronged salute, then jab the assailant in the eyes. Except, no, *no*, she doesn't NEED that, it's just her fevered mind. It's just in her head. It's just…oh, fuck it. Kirsten runs. She belts it, as fast as she's ever run, all the way home. Ah! home.

When she gets in Sam is in bed, although he sounds out of breath, like he's only just jumped in. The power must have gone down at some point, because the videos green numerals and the bedside clock's red numerals are turned to flashing Os. When she undresses, the room is lit up like a crime scene. "So how's your mental state?" Sam asks, slurringly, fumbling at Kirsten's body as though it is running target, a chase, when she is only lying very still. Suddenly sober. The realisation hits her that she feels nothing but anger towards him, in his cloying goodness. No, that's a lie - she does feel something more. Something close to hate.

This is so wrong.

She only has to say those two words, the words she planned earlier - *you're dumped* - and it will all be over: the relationship, the walk, the road.

Why is she afraid to say *no* to these touches, when through allowing them she disgusts herself and hates him? She hates him when he has done nothing wrong, been nothing but kind, and it is *all her.*

Her nipples have shrivelled in the cold to spat-out cherry stones, and Sam takes this for arousal. "Mmm, I see you're horny too." She breathes out through her nose, a yes made of thin air. This is why she hasn't done it: money, the flat, feeling stupid. The fear. Reasons that are nothing to do with love, or passion, or him. He slips a plump finger into her arse-crack.

"I'm tired," she says.

"Come on, we've not had sex for weeks."

"I'm tired."

"You're a fucking bitch, sometimes," Sam snaps. It shocks them both, his viciousness. It is like finding broken glass in baby food.

"That wasn't very nice," she can't resist saying, as his thick body turns to face the wall.

She lies there for ages. Hours. Soon the watch she has propped beside her shows 4.30. And then she sees something.

A knife, glinting on Sam's bedside table.

Ohmygodohmygodohmygod.

The knife. The way he snapped. His quick breathing. The fact that it was *him* who said the robbery was in her head. The way he's been so 'there for her.' The way the stress has driven her to need him more. The bedroom window that is *–holy shit! --* wide open. His completely unconvincing level of niceness.

141

It occurs to Kirsten she is sleeping with a cunning, manipulative psychopath.

A psychopath with a fucking big pointy KNIFE!

It is a horror movie:

Tonight, Kirsten Woolly stars IN
My Psysho-Killer Boyfriend Blood Bath!
Directed by: Nate Twist.

Wasting no time, Kirsten leaps out of bed, grabs the knife, grabs the bedside lamp and is about to bring it down on his head when he screeches and, with the strength of a *mad man* goddamit, leaps up and pushes her to the floor. He tries to grab the knife and they struggle. She kicks his bollocks. He yelps. He elbows her tit. She pokes two fingers in his eyes. If only he had an earring! She kicks his bollocks again, instead. "AAAAAGGGGGGHHHHH!" Sam screams, and she takes her chance, grabs the knife up, pulls on her dressing gown and runs.

She runs all the way to the police station opposite the bus stop, and sobbing, tells her story.

Oh, did I not tell you? Sam is possibly the nicest person in the world. He works for Amnesty and Childline in his spare time. He always carries a Bag-for-Life shopping bag, to avoid unnecessary environmental damage. In his holidays he takes disabled kids on adventure holidays. Disliking him is the moral equivalent of Holocaust denial or standing as a BNP candidate.

The knife was a cheese knife he'd bought for his grandma's birthday the next day, and not yet wrapped.

Now he will never be able to have children, and has to keep a look out for glaucoma.

Being nice, he did not press charges on Kirsten, on the condition she left the city.

And now? Kirsten Woolly lives in suburbia. She has one child, another on the way, an aga and a Land Rover, and has become an Avon lady in her spare time. Last week, she bought a 24-piece Tupperware set.

I warned you it was not a happy ending.

This city breaks people.

Clocks and Faces
Tony Sides

The two of them talked quietly in bed, in the dark with the red numbers of the radio alarm clock lighting the edge of the bedside cabinet, their voices soft and close and faces unseen in that night-time intimacy of couples which for them, when they first slept together and then lived together, was so lovely and the opposite of loneliness.

And was a surprise to both of them, who until then through their lives had always hidden so many of their feelings secretly and thoroughly and even from themselves behind those words and that behaviour expected or required by family and teachers, and that could cover all the thoughts that made them feel different and uncertain.

So this intimacy, voices relaxed and slow and yawny, secrets painlessly told, had been exciting and a comfort. When the sex had disappointed one or both of them and made them feel separate and worried, the talking had made them happy and made them hopeful enough to give the sex another chance next time. However tired they were in those days they had talked for hours, not needing sleep, feeling as if they got their rest from being in the dark and from the warm skin of his long gaunt body being against the warm skin of her heaviness, accepting each other's appearance, faces close together, breathing together, whispering and laughing sometimes, and moving their relationship further stages forward with the talking.

The things they hid from themselves they could not talk about. Those were just left as lonelinesses, pushed a long way down and never looked at directly.

Many of the things they did discuss were difficult to bring up, mostly because of the people they were, rather than the things themselves, but there was a feeling of how much of this can the other one stand me to admit?; and of course much of the conversation was trying to guess what the other one wanted to hear, what was the right answer to give?

They each kept a lot of their feelings private. But the speaking of what they could relax enough to speak about was lovely for them both.

That had changed. This bed-time quiet talking could still be a comfort after difficult days at work, but now they talked for less time and turned more quickly away to think or try to sleep. They treated it more as a time to complain, or worry, or make practical plans about trips or shopping.

Tonight he started talking about plans for his parents to visit them at Xmas, and she turned over in bed, and started kissing him to end the conversation.

He had been out with a friend in the afternoon six weeks ago and they had been having quite a good time, although the day had not been as structured as he would have liked.

He would probably have enjoyed it more with a friend who was more similar to him and more organized and steady. He had been quiet and tired after a week at work and his friend had been laughing and quick-moving. He thought his friend would have liked it to be one long, unhurried round of eating and drinking and markets and art galleries and record stores, and second-hand-book shops; whereas he had wanted to visit places in the most efficient order and for a defined purpose, and had limited their time by looking at his watch and sighing, or standing still waiting, trying to hurry his friend psychically. But it had still been all right. The Xmas lights were already up.

After the gallery, where his friend had only wanted to see the impressionists and Van Gogh, they had gone for a coffee in the cafe in the crypt under that church with the blue clock-face. Leaving his friend in the cafe chatting to some thin-hipped red-haired woman he knew, he had nipped upstairs in to the sunshine and tourist- and traffic-noise to try to find a phone box that was empty.

He had noticed the two cards while he was ringing the rail inquiries number to check the train times for the evening.

There had been other prostitute cards blu-tacked inside the phone box but the two in front of him had been different. They had been glossy and postcard-sized and each had a black-and-white photo of a woman with lettering above and below it on a brightly-coloured background. Looking at them he had felt his face flush and as if he was going to start shaking.

"1800 arrives 18.44," the Scottish man had told him over the phone.

He had gone back to the front of the church carrying his jacket over his arm to cover his hand, which was holding the two cards. When he had seen that his friend was on his own outside the church, he had said, "I found these in the phone box. They've both got 07000 numbers on them." He had felt that he was giving himself an alibi somehow.

"Well spotted," his friend had said. "They're not alphadial, though."

"They might spell something. 07000 FOR-A-FUCK?"

"No," his friend had said, giving the cards back. "They've both got ones and zeros in them, and there are no letters on those keys."

They had waited to cross the road, and then walked across.

"Prostitutes use 07000 numbers more for the fact that you can direct them to any phone or mobile phone or whatever," his friend had said, "'without revealing your location', as we used to say in the sales pitch."

"Did you sell any to prostitutes?"

"One or two people did. The Personal Number Company cuts them off if they find out they're being used for anything like that."

"What does this mean? On the 18-year-old student one? 'O and A levels'?"

"That's not a telecoms question," his friend had said.

He had smiled.

His friend had told him.

"Good grief," he had said.

A little further on he had asked, "Do you think these are the actual prostitutes, in the pictures?"

"No," his friend had said. "Those'll just be photos from porn mags or whatever."

He had stopped near a bin and pretended to throw the cards away, and had slid them in to the pocket of his jacket. He did not want to have sex with the prostitutes. It was only that the photographs were more explicit than anything he usually saw.

When he had got home he had looked at the cards again in the small downstairs toilet, holding them over the sink where the light was brightest.

They were both blank on the back. He had put them together with the picture-sides touching, and in to the zipped pocket of his jacket. Then he had flushed the toilet and washed his hands, and gone in to the lounge. He had taken his jacket upstairs in to the bedroom.

And tonight, now, kissing gently in the quiet dark with the red

12.02 of the radio alarm clock showing her hair faintly with her leaning over him, he could feel the smooth material of her nightie and the warmth of her body, and her eyelashes touched his skin as she kissed his open mouth.

He concentrated. The blue one had a photo of the torso of an open-mouthed Southeast Asian woman with long straight hair and huge, solid, tight-looking breasts with a blouse knotted underneath them and pulled to the sides. The lettering said Oriental Pleasure.

The red one was meant to be held lengthways, and the photo was a slim woman lying on her side leaning on one elbow and arching her back to lift her smallish breasts. She was blonde with dark eyebrows and looked about twenty-five, and she was wearing a striped tie around her bare neck. Along the top was 18 Year Old Student and the phone number, and under the photo it said O And A Levels. Accepts Discipline.

There was a slight taste of toothpaste, their faces together, kissing together, and she stopped, and pushed the straps of her nightie off her shoulders, and quicker kisses now, pressing harder, both of them.

Doppelgänger
Emma Unsworth

There's a girl over there who looks like me except her nails are longer. If I slouch in my seat I can see her knickers. They're white. A glaring triangle flanked by pasty pink.

He puts a drink in front of me and I say thanks. Good job he sees me smile. The music is so loud in here that it's impossible to talk. I wish I hadn't worn such a short skirt. I cross my legs.

She's crossed her legs now. My boyfriend has gone to the bar; the signal for people to look at me more. Not to worry. I'm looking good. I'm wearing a pink bra underneath my pink top. Bright as can be. If you can see something make a feature of it, as they say. The straps keep falling off my shoulders. It's all very seductive.

The girl who I'm sure was trying to see my knickers is on her own now. To be honest she looks a bit like me, but her boyfriend is taller than mine. His arms rest comfortably on the bar as he blows smoke at the stage. I curve a cocktail stick under my nails. So much for having a French manicure and finding a footballer. Hers over there are stubby as hell. Bitten down to the quick, as my mum would say.

A spotlight makes a false moon out of my new drink. I run my fingertips down the side of the glass, giving the condensation a carnival edge. Inside is a slice of lemon, magnified into a monster. It's my first time in here but it's also exactly my kind of place. The optics drip with cheap booze and the staff look just about ready to kill anyone who wants serving. I shout into my boyfriend's ear:

"Don't you think that girl over there looks a bit like me?"

"Don't be daft. She's blonde."

But he knows who I'm talking about. He's probably slept with her three times in his head already, and maybe even for real a few weeks ago, for all I know.

She's talking about me. I want to whisper to my boyfriend about her, but I don't know him well enough. He probably wouldn't even call himself my boyfriend yet. It's only been a few weeks. Chances are he'll take me home with him tonight, although he's starting to irritate me. When he sips his Baileys a line of cream remains on his lip for far too long. At first it was cute but I think people can overdo their own idiosyncrasies. Her bloke over there just nearly pushed her off her chair.

That was my fault but I'm alright now. I shouldn't have got into a mood. Silly, really. And he hates it when I don't tell him what's wrong. But why does he have to ogle other women so much? It's pathetic. Shit. I think she saw him push me. And the room just bulged by itself; a sure sign that I'm pissed. I'm going to the toilet.

I've got to get out of here. I think he's telling me something about the band onstage but I'm not really interested. He nudges me.

"Sorry."

"You're not listening to me, are you?"

"Yeah."

"Bloody well listen."

"Yeah."

"What?"

"Nothing. I need the toilet."

I stumble to the stairs, alongside the wailing singer overarched by a star curtain. His shock of red hair keeps beating the lights to it. A pinstripe suit vacuum packed onto his limbs and sagging a little around the chest. Cradling the microphone with his eyes squeezed tightly shut. A parody of pain. He's suffered. He's been there. Oh, yes. Now he's reaching for a reaction, eager to fall on his own pencil. It's a song about loneliness. Little wonder.

My thighs press out wide on the plastic seat. A constellation of graffiti hangs around the broken lock. Stella & Mick. Claire & Wayne. All undoubtedly together forever. Patches of lino glisten beneath me. I bring my feet together around a scrap of paper. Half of it is usable. Just about. When I'm done I open the door and she's there, leaning against the wall like a mirror.

The toilets are busting. To get out she's going to have to come really close. Her cheek is less than six inches away from mine. Skin prickles. Something clicks in my throat. I'm not sure whether she's going to kiss me or bite me. She does neither and I'm past her, in the corridor, where a gust of cold air blasts back my fringe.

157

I've climbed these stairs a thousand times. Sometimes I've skipped. Sometimes I've staggered. Now I climb. As steadily as an athlete. She'll be washing her hands. I imagine if the bar were suddenly flooded with water we'd be the only two to bob to the top.

Back upstairs I resume my post, still warm from the way she watched me all the way across the room. I glance at her, then quickly down to the crushed cigarette ends around her sandals. Her big feet are twisted and awkward-looking at the bottom of her splayed legs, like cars after a crash. Now she's putting on her jacket.

One sleeve and then the other, scruffy tassels dangling over her hands. Ready and waiting behind a full ashtray, next to a man desperate to make her fall for him. I reckon that the ends of cigarettes must fill some of the most desperate places on earth.

People are moving, spinning around the axis we've created to span this smoky hell. Before we know it, there's hardly anyone; the most lively thing left is a boy following a broom around the filthy floor, brushing bottletops into a jagged square. He does it gently, as though he's rounding up animals. Someone spits in the pile he's made. She notices too.

A taxi outside.
"That's us."
I jump at my boyfriend's voice. He's in the porch, motioning wildly. I dash out, flicking my cig on the table, leaving

her with the type of man who clenches her knee to tell her to be quiet. The type who subtly pulps her in public with a sickly sweet manner, who takes bad memories out on her in private, and who'll spend the rest of his life beating up women that remind him of his mother.

She's put ash on the table, all for the sake of a dramatic exit. For a minute I thought she was pretending to fire a gun at me but she was just tapping her fag. Dirty bitch. Not like me at all. And her black hair looks purple in the smoggy UV.

Back at his flat we get into bed and I try to forget about the dead flies on the sill and the girl in the bar. The whiskey I just slugged tasted sour, even though I picked the cleanest mug I could. My throat throbs from smoking. The lightbulb casts the shadow of a stringless violin. He kisses my ear and it sounds like a seashell; a hollow echo of somewhere I used to be. The duvet rustles and I don't want to be here. But I just can't bring myself to rise above it.

A moth fizzes repeatedly off the bare bulb; a wayward mobile on a piece of elastic. I lie like a statue, The Recumbent Frigid, wondering whether we can scrape together enough tenderness not to fuck. A plane flickers in the sky. I shut my eyes and it's gone. I open them and it's there again, transmitting down to me through the blackness in between.

A plane or a satellite curves across the sky in an invisible orbit. I squint and hold it between my fingers. The sound of the sea gets loud, so loud I'm sure I can feel it trickling down my neck to the pillow.

In the morning, yellow rays bleed through the bamboo blind. The noise of the street makes the idea of night seem far-fetched; a million miles away. My clothes lie like stepping stones to the door.

My feet make ticking noises on the floor. I hear the paper arrive, heavy with supplements, spilling its guts as it comes through the slot. Outside, there's a snap of winter in the air. Dry leaves scuttle across the tarmac and I kick as many as I can. A few final stars cling to their positions in the bruised clouds. I see them. Walking to the station, a bag of crisps in my sticky palm. Sycamore seeds litter the pavement like confetti and the sound of roadworks stammers through the trees. Today the sun and the moon hang simultaneously. It's a weird sight but quite a common one, I suppose.

I dive onto the tram during the beeps and sit in the concertina middle section, where the seats are singles and there aren't any windows. I hate having to see my reflection every time we go through a tunnel, and I can't help but look.

At Whitefield the doors draw back to reveal a few businessmen and then it's her, the girl from last night. Still in the pink top. Her fringe has risen into a question mark. She's holding her stomach as though she's going to be sick. There's one seat left opposite me. She folds her ballerina body into it.

I spot her instantly. Gazing at her crap shoes and tying an empty crisp packet into a knot. Me feeling as though I rattle when I walk. I sit down and her eyes burn a hole into my right side. Dead eyes. Doll's eyes. Sliding over me slowly. Look back or die. And I see the sun lighting up the loose hairs that flare off her head. She's golden. The tram hums forward and a fair way either side of her are glimpses of small things smashed up on the embankment.

I'm definitely not going to cry. But I want to when I think about how I don't want to get off this tram. And how I know she doesn't either. And how a thousand snapshots of girls like me and her are being flashed from a thousand window frames on trams screaming their way into town. But right here it's just me. And her.

I'm okay when I get to my stop. I peer out of the doorway. It's easy to get lost in a city this size. Buildings channel your way. An articulated lorry stretches to a halt, its cargo of hatchbacks huddled together like livestock. Gleaming cars queue by the platform, their drivers mute behind small screens where blades swipe them into visibility every few seconds.

The motion of the doors makes my heart skip a beat. As she whirs away I might explode. I turn. She turns. Behind her, the moon punctures the sky like a clipped fingernail.

And she's staring at me.

She's staring at me.

Decision Time
Paul Morley

I finished it.

You started it.

I was here.

You were there.

I was watching you.

You were miles away.

I was in a part of the room where there is a table and chair.

You were in another part of the room.

I had a view of the Universe that was evidently very different from the view that

You had of the Universe.

I may have seen a colour or two more or less than

You did.

I was going to sit down.

You were standing up.

I decided to sit down.

You sat down as well, in response, which oddly seemed quite threatening.

I didn't know what time of day it was.

You seemed to think it was early afternoon, although I think you were guessing, you weren't wearing a watch, not that I saw, not that I remember, and there was no clock in the room, not that I can remember, there were other things to remember, or not.

I spent the next day thinking about what happened.

You had forgotten everything.

I was tired.

You looked well, up to a point, considering, at least there was something about the way you entered the room that made me think, you look well, up to a point.

I was wearing what I usually wear, as you can imagine.

You were wearing clothes which I would describe if only I could remember them, funny that I can't remember, you made such an impression, but the only thing that I can say for certain is that you weren't naked, and your eyes were roughly the same colour as whatever it was that you wore on the top part of your body.

I will never really know exactly what happened.

You may well have been in full possession of all the facts, although I doubt it, as you can never know everything, you can never know that much really, not when you think how much there is to know, you can only know a few things from which you can work out just enough to maintain a certain, shall we say, balance, a certain pretence, or confidence, or determination, or, as the case may be, a certain indifference, you can maintain your life, which let's face it needs maintaining, not just your life, everybody's life, life needs maintaining, this is true, too true.

I was feeling a bit cold, which may or may not be relevant.

You were to all intents and purposes exactly at the right temperature you would expect given your age, sex, height and weight and the set of circumstances that had suddenly, out of nowhere, descended upon you, and I think it says a lot about my state of mind that I can calculate this.

I was thinking what to say.

You knew exactly what to say, and you said it, with some force, a force that seemed very precise, and for the first time in my life I paused to consider the way that force can be precise, a precise thing, a thing of precision; what you said was naturally forced out of you with great precision, the precision of force, the force of precision, for my benefit, although you got something from it as well, you discreetly flushed with the pleasure you felt in the precision, from the force, and the way that the two things, the force and the precision, met, in the space that joined and separated us, with great precision, and I didn't feel great, but who would.

I had something, two or three somethings, on my mind.

You guessed what was on my mind, I guess, and smiled a slight little smile that I might have misjudged, maybe it was actually friendlier than I thought, I thought you were mocking me, that you were looking down on me, that you were feeling superior, establishing your authority, but you might just have been smiling at me, you could have been saying, let's be friends, to a point, let's not be angry with each other, you could have been trying to communicate a desire to sort things out, to find peace, to get along, to agree, even if just to agree to disagree, you might have guessed wrong, I guess.

I was a couple of years older than you.

You were younger than me.

I thought I should try and catch your eye.

You looked at me straight in the eyes, and you held that look, and I took it as a challenge, to everything I was as a person, to look back, but I bet I was being too sensitive, as usual, so I'm told, and actually you were just being mature, together, calm, collected, just making sure that you maintained a measured eye contact to demonstrate that you were interested in what I was saying, in what I was going to say next, you weren't at all staring at me to intimidate me, undermine me, to unnerve me, to look at me until I looked away, which you took as a small triumph and I thought was a failure.

I looked away.

You said some words, that I almost instantly forgot, because I couldn't help but think that you were trying to annoy me, with what you said, and the way that you said it, and the way you looked at me, look, as you said it, which I sensed more than anything, because I couldn't quite look you in the eye, not for any great length, it seemed too hard, there was too much concentration involved, far too much concentration considering the fact that all we were doing, as far as you, as in someone else witnessing the pair of us in this room, the size and shape of our lives at that moment in time, the decision time, could tell, was having a conversation, that's all, up to a point.

I tried to make a point.

You smirked, I swear, smirked with contempt, you did, at what I was trying to say, you made it very clear that you thought that what I was trying to say was stupid, vague, badly thought out, and the way you looked at me, looking, made me feel more and more self-conscious, about what I was saying, and the way I was saying it, self-conscious about me as me, as what I am, if anything, you made me doubt my very existence as I tried to make my point, it wasn't as if it was about my very existence or anything, just a small point, you didn't need to provoke such doubt, I don't know how you managed it, how you made me mistrust myself, but you did, you knew what you were doing, and as I spoke, and as you smirked, I swear, my mouth dried up, my dried up mouth made the words fall apart as I tried to speak them, I thought if what I was saying made sense when I started to say it, it doesn't now, because of what you are doing to my mind, with that smirk, which is smeared lightly on top of the deep dark loathing you feel for me, and the dryness inside my mouth seemed to stretch outside of my mouth, over my lips, around my face, and it covered my whole body, and seeped into the room itself, so that the room dried up, shrank and shriveled, and the dryness spread as wide as time all the way through space miniaturising the Universe as it spread which was a hell of a thing to witness, but you stayed moist, you stayed cool, you stayed on top of things, and that made everything dry up even more, starting with my mouth and ending up way beyond comprehension, and God knows what I ended up saying, it must have been completely incoherent, and through the dryness, across the dried appalled Universe, in your isolated superior position a few feet away from the dried up me, I swear you smirked some more, you were thinking, I just know you were, how could something so dry be so wet, my mouth gave up, so dry.

I might have been seeing things the wrong way.

You seemed very sure that what you were saying was of great interest and you might well have been right, certainly your mouth seemed nicely lubricated.

I don't know what happened next.

You were in control.

I did keep trying to say something that might impress you.

You had a look in your eyes.

I wanted you to like me.

You were very polite, now I come to think of it, but I just thought it was an act, that's how I explained it to myself, you were faking it, you were going through the motions, you weren't interested in putting me at my ease or anything, I thought you were pretty abrasive actually, considering that if there had been anyone else in the room, which now I come to think of it there might have been, which is strange, as there surely wasn't, there can't have been, then to that other person you would have come across as very polite, but, no, I think you had it in for me, from the very beginning, and I think whoever else was in the room with us, they would have sensed it, been aware of it, the hostility you felt for me would not be disguised by your professional politeness, and I must try and remember if there was anyone else in the room, it must be important, maybe there was and then there wasn't, like someone time traveled in and then time traveled out, just long enough to note your hostility, maybe that's what sent them away, that actually wouldn't have been the strangest thing that happened in that room, where you were so together I just wanted to tear you apart.

I just wanted to tear you apart.

You laughed at something I said, and I wish I could say it was because I thought that you thought I had said something funny, but no, I think you laughed, at me not with me, because you felt sorry for me, you bastard, smiling at me like you think you know everything about me, like you can see right inside me, my skin is transparent, as see through as time, inside there's just a shell, a shell filled up with nothing and fear, stop looking, and your laughter was part of your power, it was the sound of your power, power that made you so powerful, power that filled you up with something and such certainty, how can I get some of that, stop laughing, stop doing that thing that you do that makes me feel the only way I can find a way out is to travel through time, into another space altogether, try laughing at that, you bastard, as I move through the time you can see through, watch me disappear, and I'll watch you disappear, stop, dead, see through dead.

I thought, but what if you are immortal, and then that would

171

make me mortal, and

You are a magician, and I am ordinary, and you are the conqueror, and I am the conquered, you are victor, I am vanquished, you are in love, and I don't have the right to be loved, and you pulled that off with just one look.

I felt that look.

You bastard.

I remember now that there was a clock in the room, but it had stopped, the hands didn't move, I kept looking at it, hoping perhaps that it might save me, save me from what I don't know, but that time could save me, I would be saved by time, I've saved so much time in my life it's here to help me, but, no, no movement, no time.

You just stopped what you were doing, what you were saying, quite by chance, I'm sure, you just stopped.   I will never forget the look on your face as I moved towards you, quite suddenly, as if I could see a situation where I might even touch you, but you weren't so sure and

You froze, an expression on your face somewhere see through, I reasoned, between real and inspired, you were inspired, and I felt good about that, good that I could inspire you, just by moving, closer towards you, moving faster than time, I was your inspiration.

I just felt that was a gentle shift in the arrangement between us, that things had changed, that there was a transference of power, or something, from where you were, to where I was, and it felt good, even as it felt not so good, or at least, at best, to be honest, a little peculiar, like it wasn't really meant to happen, like nothing was meant to happen.

You weren't so superior now.

I tried to move the conversation on, which I thought was quite brave of me, considering the way you'd turned the room with me in it to dust, the dust of me and everything around me, except you, and maybe someone else, like it was a desert, hot, empty, vast, shimmering with heat, so that just to muster up the energy to say something, just a couple of words, no great addition to the conversation we'd been having, was impressive, I thought, and surely you would have realised it if you were in a more responsive mood, that what I was saying was original, and even exciting, and worth paying serious attention to, smile like you mean it, is there someone else in the room or is that just a mirage, is there anyone there?

You didn't seem to hear me.

I saw the other person in the room, if there was one, do whatever it was they did so that they could travel though time, and I observed that dryness, silence and something mysterious just outside my field of vision seemed to be important elements in their ability to time travel, maybe they traveled into the room, which I like to think of as our room, by mistake, actually intending to travel to the 23rd century.

You were not actually able to travel through time.

I looked right at you, hard into you, into your eyes, using all the dryness in the Universe, the dryness you had caused with your power, the superpower, and I found my own power, I used it as a fuel, an energy, I made it work for me, against you, this dryness, I made it my weapon, my way of getting my way, I turned the dryness on you, you weren't expecting that, I dried you up, I did, I got you, I got you back, I got you back good and proper, you were not immortal, you were no magician, but I was a superhero, to a point, which made up for the fact that I too wasn't able to travel through time, maybe some other time, I wondered what my superhero name is, for the moment I forgot my own name let alone my made up name, I had no name, I was nameless, as nameless as

You, who don't look me in the eye anymore.

I found the words and I made a decision and I acted in time.

You went along with my decision.

I was right.

You agreed.

I had the last word.

You had no choice.

I looked forward to the next time.

You didn't.

I left the room to

You.

contributors:

Michael Bracewell is the author of six novels, the latest being *Perfect Tense* (Cape, 2001). He is a prolific journalist and his most recent non-fiction title was *The Nineties: When Surface was Depth* (Flamingo, 2002).

Wayne Clews is a regular contributor to *Attitude* and *The Gay Times*. His first short story recently appeared in *City Secrets* (Crocus, 2002).

David Constantine's poetry collections include *Madder, Watching for Dolphins, The Pelt of Wasps, Caspar Hauser,* and most recently *Something for the Ghosts*. He is a translator of Hölderlin, Brecht, Goethe, Kleist, Enzensberger, Michaux and Jaccottet.

Amanda Dalton's radio plays include *I Think I Could Turn and Live with Animals*. Her first collection of poetry *How to Disappear* (Bloodaxe) was shortlisted for the 1999 Forward First Book Award.

Shelagh Delaney wrote *A Taste of Honey* (1960) at the age of 17, and a year later *The Lion in Love*. She has since published a collection of short stories, *Sweetly Sings the Donkey*, and has written widely for TV, radio and cinema. Her screenplays include *The White Bus* (1966), *Charlie Bubbles* (1968) and *Dance With a Stranger* (1985).

Tariq Mehmood co-directed *Injustice*, a feature documentary dealing with deaths in police custody which won the 2002 Black Film Maker Best Documentary Award. His first novel *Hand on the Sun*, was published by Penguin in 1983. He also writes in Pothowari, his mother tongue, and is a founder of the Pothowari-Pahari language movement which aims to develop a script to enable the language to be written down.

Paul Morley has been a writer and columnist for the *NME, The Face, Blitz, The New Statesman, The Guardian* and *Esquire*. He was an original presenter of BBC2's *The Late Show* and a founding member of the group Art of Noise. His first book, *Nothing*, was published by Faber in 2000.

Jeanie O'Hare's fiction has appeared in *The Diva Book of Short Stories* (MPG, 2001). She was the recipient of a Jerwood Foundation Bursary in 1999.

Ra Page (ed) founded the *Manchester Stories* magazine series, and edited *The City Life Book of Manchester Short Stories* (Penguin, 1999). He has written for *The Guardian, The Times* and *The New Statesman*, and was a recipient of a Jerwood Foundation Bursary in 1999. He is Deputy Editor of *City Life*.

Clare Pollard wrote most of her first collection of poetry, *The Heavy-Petting Zoo* (Bloodaxe, 1998) whilst still at school. She has since written and narrated a programme for Channel 4, *The Sixteenth Summer*, and published a second collection: *Bedtime* (Bloodaxe, 2002). She is currently working for *The Idler* magazine, and writing her first novel *Monsters*.

Gwendoline Riley's first novel *Cold Water* (Cape, 2002) won the 2002 Betty Trask Prize for a First Novel.

Tony Sides has previously published fiction in the magazine, *Multi-Story*.

Michael Symmons Roberts is the author of three collections of poetry, *Soft Keys*, *Raising Sparks* and last year's *Burning Babylon*. He is also an award winning documentary producer for the BBC.

Anthony Wilson's first piece of fiction, 'The Lightweight Trigger' was published anonymously in *The City Life Book of Manchester Short Stories* (Penguin, 1999). He has since written a novelisation of Michael Winterbottom's film *Twenty-Four Hour Party People* (2002).

Gerard Woodward is the author of three award-winning collections of poetry, *Householder, After the Deafening* and *Island to Island*. His first novel *August* was shortlisted for the Whitbread First Novel Prize 2001.

Emma Unsworth is a graduate of Manchester University's Novel Writing MA.

acknowledgements:

Five of the stories included here were originally commissioned for two limited-issue short story supplements, *Manchester Stories* parts 3 and 4, published in association with *City Life* magazine. Thanks to Bron Williams and Eunice Toh at NWAB, Jon Atkin at Waterstone's, and Ric Michael for help in the production of these. Special thanks are also due to Steve Moyler, Marcus Graham, Isaac Shaffer, Laura Dixon, Sarah Tierney and Lin & Jon; also to Angharad, Joyce, Judith, Pam and Michael at Carcanet Press, and everyone at *City Life*, especially LBB.... you guys!